For my family. Despite what Piers Black
would have us believe, they mean the world to me.

'In a world so concerned at the same time with environmental issues and financial gain, Piers Black is a compelling anti-hero for our times. The Profit is a serious, and at times painfully funny, short book that carries a valuable message.'

MARTIN OUVRY

Martin Ouvry is a novelist and writer of short stories. He is an editor with The Writers' Workshop (and previously The Literary Consultancy) and has reviewed books for The Sunday Times and The Observer.

Roast Books

GREAT LITTLE READS

This paperback edition first published in 2008 by
Roastbooks Ltd.
No. 31, 93 Albert Embankment, London, SE1 7TY
www.roastbooks.co.uk

A catalogue record of this book is available from the British Library

ISBN: 978-1-906894-03-0

THE PROFIT

JOHN KARTER

Thank you to everyone who believed in The Profit, especially Faye Dayan and everyone at Roastbooks, my agent Serafina Clarke, and Martin Ouvry, without whose encouragement and editorial guidance this book would probably still be languishing in a drawer of my desk.

Piers the Powerful, revered by men and universally desired by women, a legend in his own Armani suit, had waited fifteen long minutes outside the fifty-storey office block for the chauffeur-driven limousine that was to carry him to the meeting of the shareholders in the financial heartland of the City. As he stood outside the soaring edifice that towered over London's Isle of Dogs like some vast spaceship from the outer realms of the cosmos, and watched the sleek black limousine purring towards him through the streets teeming with traffic and office workers, he paused for a moment to consider the task that lay before him, and his heart was filled to overflowing with a singular kind of joy.

As Piers descended the steps, his diamond-encrusted Rolex glinting in the sunlight, he looked out past the sprawl of office buildings and across the vast expanses of the River Thames and a far-off look appeared in his eye. Reaching with irritation for his mobile phone, which had begun to sing out its familiar little tune as yet another well-wisher called to offer sycophantic words of encouragement, he muttered a few terse words, summarily put an end to the call, and thrust it back into the silk-lined pocket of his suit.

After stooping momentarily to wipe away a speck of dust, which had settled on one of his immaculate Gucci loafers, his gaze was caught by a pigeon pecking hungrily at a crust thrown by an elderly woman clutching a bag of stale bread to her bosom. As he watched the bird suddenly take flight and disappear into the skies, his mind began to carry him back to the days of his childhood. And as the rumble of a train passing close by shook him from his reverie, he was seized by an all-consuming feeling of sadness that momentarily eclipsed the burgeoning sense of *joie de vivre* in his soul.

As he continued to descend the steps he brushed hard against the old woman, sending her tumbling to the ground and scattering her bag of bread across the pavement like giant snowflakes. Ignoring her bitter cries of remonstration, as she attempted slowly and painfully to lift herself to her feet, he refocussed his mind on sealing the execution of his latest and greatest takeover, visualising how he would present it to the meeting with complete conviction and authority despite the opposition of those cursed few who had sworn to depose him as Chairman and Chief Executive.

For, he told himself as his limousine made painfully slow progress through the traffic towards him, whatever the personal feuds and settling of old scores underlying this monumental corporate coup, and independent of the fact that it affords me the opportunity to swell my personal fortune many times over, is it not true that I am fulfilling my duty to place before the shareholders the very best opportunities for growth and prosperity?

And though she who read my future from the cards foretold that it would not be with a carefree heart that I will address the meeting, but with a heaviness and a prescience of trouble bubbling through my soul, I will not be swayed for one instant from my chosen path. And though I may feel the sting of bitter opposition before those of limited vision comprehend the implications of the resolution I bring before them, yet still am I at peace with myself. I, of all people, know only too well that true strength is forged in the furnace of adversity, and therefore it is a good thing that they test me in this way.

How is it that I have come this far and stand poised to become the richest man in all of the United Kingdom, featured more on the cover of *Fortune* magazine than even Rupert Murdoch or Richard Branson? Was it not by the sweat of my exquisitely-toned body and the insight of my rapier-like mind that I clawed my way from office junior to the most powerful, most commercially aware, most envied, most desired man in London?

Many were the nights when I lay fatigued to the point of desperation at my desk, knowing that I must rise to greet the challenge of a new dawn, even though my brain was aching from the knife-edge manoeuvrings of the previous day's trading. And now, as I reap the princely rewards of a business empire that increases daily and is making its presence felt in all four corners of the globe, I know that I shall not leave the meeting today without scars from bitter rivals. Yet though I am mistrusted and misunderstood by those with infinitely less inspiration, I know also, as certainly as the Thames reaches out to the mighty ocean, that when the cut and thrust of battle is ended I will emerge infinitely more powerful and revered.

For my ways are not the ways of ordinary, pinstriped city men. My ways are the ways of Onassis, Trump and Getty, yet even more unerring and irresistible than theirs, for the inner light that guides my path towards domination of world markets on an unprecedented scale has not even begun to reach its full magnitude. Given that I have walked for a mere thirty years on this earth, and only a third of those have been given over to honing the innate skills and qualities of the ultimate entrepreneur and tycoon, I am but a weanling in relative terms. If I have accomplished this much in my commercial infancy, how much more will I achieve when my business brain has begun to maximise its potential?

And as his limousine with the personalised number plate PRO 4IT pulled up at the foot of the steps, and the chauffeur doffed his cap and opened the door for him, he berated the fawning fellow for his lateness and informed him that his job was hanging by a thread. As the chauffeur began to grovel and spewed out a series of excuses about his heart condition playing up again, about his young son being taken ill and rushed into hospital, and about the severity of the traffic, Piers harangued him even more, telling him that he was a pathetic specimen, and that time was money, and money was the *sine qua non* of life, and that a life lived to the full was a healthy interplay between the management of time and the accumulation, investment and spending of ever greater sums of money.

As the limousine pulled away, and he settled back in his seat and poured himself a drink from the elegant walnut cocktail cabinet, he switched on the television set. And as he flicked through the channels and saw the huge rise in the price of his company's shares on the screen in front of him, he felt his senses soar like the pigeon surging skyward moments earlier. And he knew in his heart that he would find the inspiration to win over those who heard his words that afternoon and fire them up to take on the challenge of his latest and most audacious takeover bid. And he knew, just as certainly, that he would squash the efforts of his enemies, as surely as the elephant crushes the dung beetle beneath its pounding feet.

For what is failure, he asked himself, but the spineless surrender of a man who has relinquished every scintilla of pride and resigned himself to wallow in the mire of self pity? Often have I felt the sting of Machiavellian manoeuvring and inhaled the stench of double dealing, but still have I clung to my over-riding belief that a man can be anything he wants to be, provided he believes in the very fibre of his being that he is destined for greatness.

Yet as he contemplated the spoils of victory, imagining the cheers of his supporters ringing in his ears, and calculated a further mammoth increase in the value of his personal shareholding, he felt his heart grow heavy again. Why is it, he asked himself, that even as I stand on the threshold of one of the most stunning commercial triumphs ever seen in the western world, I am forced once again to face the demons of my birthright?

For, as Sartre has said, a man is whatever he chooses to be, not an eternal slave to his circumstances. Yet as the eagle returns to its eyrie, so my thoughts are destined forever to drag me back to the bear-pit of my humble origins, just a stone's throw across the waters in the bowels of the East End. For, even though I have long ago left behind those squalid beginnings, still I hear the plaintive, tortured cries of my father, now on his second heart bypass, my mother, racked with arthritis, and my five brothers and four sisters condemned to labour eternally in the family drapery business, their only glimmer of salvation being the hope of a swift and merciful end to their misery.

Yet as they toil from dawn till dusk like prisoners in a chain gang, and I enjoy the feted, cosseted lifestyle of a pop star or an oil-rich Arab prince, how can I change their unrelenting tunnel vision and lift them from their self-inflicted misery? And why should it even cross my mind to concern myself with people whose imagination extends no further than those very walls that cage them and whose sense of the good life is limited to a day at

Bognor Regis and jellied eels and whelks for tea? In this dog-eat-dog world it is every man for himself, and it is I who, by my own unstinting efforts and nobody else's, have opened wide the gates of opulence and let the life-giving waters flow over me like milk and honey.

As he sat back in his limousine, sipping his Martini and nibbling a mouthful of best Beluga caviar, he peered out through the tinted windows at the lunchtime crowds busily making their way through the City streets and focussed for an instant on a hunched old man with flowing grey hair and round pebble glasses. And though he denied it to himself, a solitary tear rolled from his eye, ran down the entire length of his cheek and plopped gently into his Martini, for the old man had momentarily reminded him of his father, and he became aware that he had not spoken to him for two long years.

Draining the remains of his drink in one swift movement, Piers smoothed his outlandishly expensive silk tie, then reached for his mobile but, before he had finished dialling his father's number, replaced it in his pocket. Oh, powerful and all-knowing one, he told himself, expunging the image of the old man from his consciousness, remember the mental muscle and the steely resolve on which you have built your empire.

For what may it profit a man to indulge in nostalgia and sentiment if it means for one second taking his mind off the more vital matters of commercial expediency? That way lies the slippery slope to damnable compromise, to the yoke of fair and reasonable negotiation, to the unspeakable curse of stating that your word is your bond and meaning it, and ultimately to the creeping paralysis of lower profits, lower dividends for shareholders and a personal fortune that is not all it might possibly be.

My conscience is as clear as the night sky over Africa, he told himself. For have I not been magnanimous in the extreme in my dealings with my family? Have I not offered them financial assistance in exchange for what I considered to be quite reasonable levels of manual work, and did I not advise them to purchase shares when the company was still in its infancy and even offered to secure them loans to purchase the shares? What is more, I stated that I would intervene personally should the money-lenders send in their men to take away their worldly goods, in the event of them being unable to keep up the repayments, insisting that they remove their shoes when entering their houses and demanding they take special care when loading the items onto their lorry.

For, truly, my generosity knows no bounds, and my concern for the well-being of my fellow men is of saintly proportions. Do I not give regularly to charity, not just trifling amounts but the kind of sums that would buy me a bottle of vintage Bollinger, or a three-course meal at Le Gavroche? And have I not indulged many of my employees in their continuing incompetence, keeping them on the payroll on vastly-reduced salaries, when dismissal without compensation would have been fully merited? Such unwavering selflessness has made me what I am today, for a man reaps what he sows, and I have gathered only the first fruits of my magnanimity, and as my largesse continues unabated, there is so much more to come.

And as the limousine edged its way slowly through the traffic, Piers exhorted his chauffeur to ignore all traffic lights and one-way signs, and scatter pedestrians with the utmost aggression. The chauffeur began to sweat profusely and asked if he might stop the car for a moment to take one of his angina pills. And Piers cursed him for his lack of consideration and told him that the meeting of the shareholders was infinitely more important in the overall scheme of things than a little bout of angina. As the barely-conscious driver clutched his chest with his left hand, whilst clinging grimly to the steering wheel with his right hand, Piers glanced anxiously at his watch and began to calculate exactly how much, if anything, he should leave him in his pay packet that week.

As their destination loomed into view, Piers mixed himself another Martini and felt the adrenalin coursing through his veins as his moment of destiny drew nigh. Making one last brief call on his mobile, to remind his secretary of their celebratory post-meeting tryst in his suite at the Dorchester that evening, he sat back and contemplated the scenario that would ensue after he delivered the *coup de grace*, and sent the opposition spinning like a heavyweight boxer crashing to the canvas after a knockout blow.

The limousine reached the building and drew up to the kerb, and as the chauffeur staggered round to open Piers' door and collapsed on the pavement, hordes of paparazzi streamed forward, and cameras popped and clicked like a presidential photo call at The White House. And as Piers stepped from the car, brushed down the lapels of his suit and smoothed back his hair, he walked casually over the fallen chauffeur, hardly noticing the man's agonised gasps and wheezes, and stood by the door of the building posing for the photographers, with the smile of a winner who knows he was born to carry all before him.

As the reporters closed in like a pack of hungry wolves and began to fire questions at him, a stunningly beautiful young woman approached, eased her way through the crowd and draped herself around him like a boa constrictor entwining itself around its prey. Mr Black, she sighed, for so long I have been your greatest admirer. If you only knew how I respect your incredible business acumen and your calculated ruthlessness. I adore you; I worship the ground you stand upon. I want to make love to you.

And Piers looked her up and down coolly and said: What's in it for me? Then he pushed her brusquely aside and told her to ring his secretary, to be put on the waiting list. Turning to the baying mob of journalists, he smiled enigmatically and said: I have no comment to make at this time. For, he told himself, the less a man says, the more he brings to himself an aura of mystery, and the more his enemies fear the secrets he keeps locked within his mind. A true tycoon's gaze is always fixed immovably on his next major deal; he has no truck with idle chatter and gossip; his thoughts are not for public consumption, except when he offers a carefully calculated morsel to tease and intrigue and lull the opposition into a false sense of security.

With a theatrical wave of his hand, he turned on his heel and made his way inside the building, where a dozen of his minions awaited him with the latest news and rumours from the market. And one of them, a bright-eyed young man with an eager manner and a spring in his step, leapt forward clutching a piece of paper with the projected voting figures and ventured to comment that everything looked set fair for the takeover to be approved. And Piers prodded the young man in his chest with his finger repeatedly and told him: Complacency is the mother of defeat, and baseless optimism is the gateway to penury. Never read the last rites over your enemies until they are cold in the ground. For men of commerce are the most devious and cunning of all, and their capacity for plunging the knife in when your guard is down knows no bounds.

Yet is not the young fellow right, he asked himself as he walked on imperiously. For there is no other way of thinking but to be unyieldingly positive. Even to consider for one nanosecond the possibility of defeat is like the first manifestation of a cancer that takes hold gradually and eats away at the body until it cannot be stopped. And I am not an ordinary man of flesh and blood. Yes, I can be wounded in physical terms, but my spirit does not feel pain or grow fatigued in any mortal sense and, being housed in my Adonis-like body, which is a temple to all that is best in masculinity, it has the perfect resting place to restore itself if there is even a hint of creeping negativity.

Feeling his inner certitude growing by the second, he walked on, followed by a phalanx of advisers, well-wishers and hangers-on, who had attached themselves to the rest so they could cloak themselves in his aura and feel a part, if only for one brief moment, of his impending triumph. And as he walked, he snapped his fingers and demanded coffee and cognac and the finest Havana cigars from eager minions, who launched themselves off in various directions to do his bidding almost before the words had left his lips.

Then he gestured to his jacket and instantly a man appeared with a clothes brush and began to brush him down as he continued to make his way to the meeting hall. And a manicurist began to file and fuss over his nails, and another young woman expertly applied make-up to his handsome face to ensure he looked his charismatic best in the glare of the spotlight and the probing lenses of the television cameras.

Then, as he turned the corner, an old woman, with the dark and brooding features of a Romany queen, loomed suddenly into view. As she began to approach him, he recognised her as the one who had read the cards and warned him of the conflict he must face if he was to force the takeover through. But even before he could summon his minders to dismiss her from his presence, she spoke. Beware the one who knows you best of all, she hissed through teeth that were as blackened and broken as a burnt-out building after the Blitz. For though you have already defeated your enemies in your mind and scattered their resistance to the winds, yet there is one who comes who knows your deepest secret and will exploit it to the full before the clock has chimed thrice.

And as his burly minders flexed their muscles and lifted the woman up and carried her, cackling and screaming, towards the outer door of the building, Piers stopped in his tracks and his features suddenly became contorted with horror. Cursing audibly, he snatched the clothes brush from the minion's hand and hurled it to the floor. Then he pushed the manicurist and the make-up girl violently away, sending them spinning against the walls.

For it was not the words of the Romany woman alone that had stirred such a sense of foreboding in him, but the sight of a frail hunched figure making his way haltingly towards him from the other end of the corridor. As he shuffled along slowly with the aid of a walking stick, Piers knew without a shadow of a doubt the identity of the man looming ever closer like some ghostly chimera. The long, flowing grey hair, the thick pebble glasses, the old, familiar, badly fitting suit, and, if anything, the brow a little more furrowed than he remembered – everything about the man confirmed his worst fears. Impossible though it seemed, the apocalyptic figure was none other than his father.

But how in the name of Bill Gates could he have got in here, he asked himself. How could my father have obtained access to this building, when security is tighter than at a presidential summit meeting? Was it really him, or was it an apparition sent to haunt him? The answer was swift in coming, as the old man moved closer, pointed at him with his walking stick and fixed him with his steely gaze.

So the irresistible Piers is set to become even mightier, the old man rasped in a slow but surprisingly strong voice. How many more millions will you make today, my oh so cunning and devious son? And when you take this latest company over, how many more hapless people will you put out of their jobs as callously as a small boy picks the wings off a butterfly? And will you spare a thought for their families as you compile the hit list, or will you simply be calculating the extra profit margins with that cold and clinical brain of yours?

Fear, primitive and uncontrollable, ran up Piers' spine like ice-water. He fingered the knot of his tie anxiously, motioned his acolytes to step back and then wandered hesitantly over to speak to him.

So, my ancient and forever whingeing Father – he choked momentarily on the word – you would seek to embarrass and belittle me by your presence. But know you, old man, that you have no right to be here. I could have you thrown out bodily, as a kitchen hand throws a piece of meat to the dogs. This meeting is for shareholders and company personnel alone, he said, his confidence returning as he scrutinized his father's stooped and dishevelled appearance. Family ties, if that is the proper expression in our case, count for nothing; for though we may be linked by some unfortunate biological accident, our ways are as different as silk and sackcloth.

But enough, old man. My words are not to be cast meaninglessly as pearls before swine, so I tell you now, and I will not say it again: if you have come to cause trouble then leave now before you fall prey to my security men, who would strike you down and expel you from the building, as they would a cheap crook or a sleazy tabloid reporter.

Yes, I will go, but mark you well, I *will* be back, his father replied in a voice replete with emotion. And all your security men, and all your fawning popinjays, and your own high and mighty ways will come to nought when I unmask you for the cold-hearted devil that you really are. For even in your callous indifference you have spoken the truth: you are indeed no son of mine. I have five real sons, who have worked tirelessly for me all their lives, and they are honourable and decent men and would not stoop as low as you if they were beaten within an ace of their lives. Yes, I will go now for it grieves me to stand in the presence of one who has eschewed the obligations of his birth and become nothing less than a travesty of a man. But keep your guard up, perfidious Piers, for this frail old man you now deny will bring you to your knees, even before your latest confidence trick is signed and sealed.

Begone, old man, you bore me, Piers said, turning on his heel and waving away his security men who had moved in like piranhas scenting blood. Let him be, he is merely a pathetic bag of wind, he told them. His empty words cannot harm me. And he walked on to the end of the corridor and into the hall where the meeting was to take place. And as the flash bulbs popped and the television cameras zoomed in, he smiled and acknowledged the applause with no visible sign of the traumatic encounter from which he had just emerged.

Yet as he took his seat beneath the portraits of many great men of commerce and industry in the ancient hall, a growing sense of turmoil gripped him from within, and his angst would not be assuaged, and he began to sweat, and his face turned a sickly pale. One of his fellow board members asked him if there was anything wrong, and he snapped at the man and told him that everything was under control, but in his heart he knew that it was not. For his father's words and those of the old gypsy woman were bedevilling his thinking and eating away at his senses like acid.

And as he sat at the front of the hall, perspiring ever more freely under the glare of the spotlights, the shareholders began to funnel their way into the room. And as the seats began swiftly to fill up, and the hall became abuzz with animated conversation and an almost tangible air of expectation, he wondered in his heart if he would find the strength to carry through his masterplan when the time came to deliver. For he was beginning to feel physically, as well as mentally debilitated, to the point of virtual paralysis, and it was a feeling that in all his days of dominance he had never experienced before, and the more it crept over him the more he felt gripped by fear and panic.

As the meeting was called to order, and the last remaining seats were filled, he heard his name being called as if in a dream, 'Ladies and gentlemen, please welcome your Chairman, Piers Black… ' The voice seemed to tail off as he found himself rising to his feet, with applause ringing in his ears. As the clapping and cheering reached a crescendo, some remained silent and kept their hands by their sides, but the groundswell of approval at his name far outweighed the token protests. And as he sensed the wave of adulation sweeping through the hall, he found himself emerging from the stupor that had threatened to immobilise him, and he looked out across the sea of approving faces and knew in his heart that he would carry all before him – as he always had and always would.

Whilst he waited for the people to be seated again, he noticed a woman remain standing three rows from the front. Her eyes were like sapphires of the deepest blue, and she possessed the finely chiselled features of one of noble birth. She fixed him with her gaze, waiting until every last shareholder had taken their seat, before addressing him. And he looked at her with great fondness, for he recognised her as one who had spoken fervently in his favour at previous meetings, on one occasion swaying the vote his way when the hawks appeared to have put his takeover plans into disarray. And as he felt her benign presence wafting over him, he knew with absolute certainty that she was the harbinger of good fortune and victory.

As a hush descended over the meeting, the one called Alexandra, who besides being a business woman of extraordinary acumen was a mystic and a visionary, spoke in a voice as unwavering as the rush of the mighty river to the sea. And she revered him, saying: Oh, Piers the Powerful, great and mighty ruler of our vast commercial cosmos, deliverer of our company from the jaws of marauding predators, magnanimous controller of our destiny and maker of incomparable corporate wealth for those who are fortunate enough to have you as their leader and guide. Long have you laboured to bring us to this day of destiny when our corporation will at a stroke become the single most powerful commercial entity in the western world. Yet I know that deep in your heart there is sorrow and a longing to break free from the shackles of your past so that you may fulfil the role you were truly created for, and I know, too, that there is so much more to the essence of your greatness than mere commercial genius.

So as we approach this momentous time, we commit ourselves

to your unerring hands. Be our mentor and our guide, oh all-seeing one; lead us to frontiers previously uncrossed and to triumphs hitherto unthought of. And as we stand on the cutting edge of destiny, pour forth your wisdom to us; and even though we are not worthy to wipe the dust from your personal organiser, reveal to us your truth, a truth that will change the course of history and bring men of spurious power to their knees. Edify us, oh master of the financial universe. Speak to us of profit.

And as Alexandra took her seat, Piers felt the glow of self-satisfaction washing over him, and he stood bold and upright with the confidence of one who knows his name has already been written in the book of immortality. And as he surveyed the sea of expectant faces, each one trained unwaveringly on him, he told himself: Though I have said with good reason in the past that my words of wisdom are not to be cast like pearls before swine, to provide succour for my less-gifted peers and ammunition for my enemies, yet will I reveal to them at least a modicum of the reasoning behind my genius.

For as well as being the most brilliant businessman this planet has ever seen, do I not also have an intellect equal to that of any Oxford don, and am I not a wit and raconteur of extraordinary talent and a communicator of unparalleled effectiveness? And as this is my day, and I hold the world of commerce in my exquisitely manicured hands, a gift of insight freely offered can only add to my reputation.

So, he told them, you would have me speak to you of profit, yet at one level you already know everything there is to know. If you could unlock the vast treasury of your unconscious you would realise you do not need mere words to convince you that profit is the fire that kindles life itself. Yet at the moment of revelation, when your inner voice asserts that you are nothing without the heady scent of the profit motive to drive you on, you hesitate like sheep at the edge of a precipice, scared to leap into the void yet sensing implicitly that in the very act of risking all you will find the answer to your ultimate longing.

For what is it to lust after profit but to seek the one true prize in a world where winners take everything worth having, and losers are no better than dead men walking? What is it to suffer the scorn of those who see profit as a dirty word, but to reveal to them the glorious truth of our very existence? And what would it profit a man to gain his soul, but let the whole world slip through his fingers?

Profit is the lifeblood that courses through your veins; it is the hope that sustains you in your darkest hour. Profit makes visionaries of those who would seek its eternal power and lifts them beyond the realms of ordinary corporate achievers into the pantheon of business immortals. And whilst oysters, Spanish fly and little blue pills may do it for some, let me tell you from personal experience that profit is the greatest aphrodisiac you will ever find.

Furthermore, ask yourselves this: is it not an indisputable truth that the tycoon surveying his ever-increasing wealth experiences an inner peace far greater than any navel-gazing guru? And the commodity dealer, contemplating vast fortunes as the tide of world trade swings in his favour – does he not feel a surge of pure adrenalin spinning his senses round like a line of the finest cocaine? And what of bankers, estate agents and lawyers – do they not feel one step closer to the spark of life itself as they watch their profits soar to even greater levels? And even the local shopkeeper tallying up his takings in pounds and pence – does he not feel he has accessed his only true *raison d' être*?

And though it is true, as the advertisements warn, that investments can go down as well as up, what bold new horizons would life offer without the lure of soaring profits and the promise of ever-increasing share prices? What hope would there be for faithful but unmotivated employees without the potential for vast new sources of wealth to enrich their dull and unfulfilling lives? Though the true entrepreneur eschews safety and sets his sights on high-risk ventures far above the daily interplay of corporate dealing, is it not true that the worst crime against working people is a company which fails to operate at a profit?

You would ask me for the secret of my own extraordinary genius for profit, even though each one of you sees me standing before you, a man like any other. I eat, I sleep, I bleed, but you know that your eyes deceive you, that this is not the full extent of my consummate commercial being. Yet to offer you the insight of one who seeks, and will undoubtedly gain, nothing less than world domination of the commercial sector, would be to steal the fire from your own bellies and rob your spirit of its knowing.

For he who turns to others more successful than himself as role models for his own progress on the graph of profitability will flounder as certainly as a fishing boat lashed against the rocks. And the fool who would attempt to steal the secrets and the guile of one more innately blessed with those characteristics will be hunted down by the forces of retribution as surely as a murderer who forgets to wipe his fingerprints from the smoking gun.

It is the hunger lurking deep within the breast pocket of your finest Savile Row suit that will carry you to your goal, as unerringly as an arrow speeds towards its target; the single-mindedness throbbing beneath the bonnet of your Rolls Royce Silver Shadow that will drive you on to balance sheets writ in letters of gold; the vision shining through the cockpit of your personalised Lear Jet that will spur you to heady new levels of turnover.

For it is only in your capacity for trampling on your competitors like ants that you will find the incomparable high of commercial dominance. And only when you have tasted the fruits of your own self-serving endeavours and revelled in the birth-pangs of new enterprises ruthlessly conceived and undertaken, will you know the joy of true creation. And as your mind breaks free of the financial chains surrounding it and loosens itself from the yoke of honourable thinking, you will savour the inner contentment of a destiny rightfully attained and rise up to claim the prize of profit unlimited.

And as he paused to seek the nodding affirmation of those who truly understood his transcendental wisdom, a pinstriped one from the midst of the grey masses assembled throughout the great hall rose to his feet and said: Oh, Mighty One, speak to us now of greed.

And he smiled, saying: What is there that I can tell you of greed that you have not already seen for yourselves? For in the mere presence and ascendancy of man on this earth you have witnessed the protective, all-providing nature of greed. Just as Darwin himself postulated the survival of the fittest, so the innate voraciousness of man for that which belongs to his father, his brother, his colleague and his neighbour is the very essence of his existence.

As the admirable Gordon Gekko said in that most edifying of movies, Wall Street, greed is indeed good. Without greed, would not man be paralysed by a creeping stasis that would leave him open to the most dastardly deeds of his fellows? And without the inherent drive to possess more and more, and store up riches in Swiss bank accounts, and salt away in vaults objects of beauty and rarity, would he not be as the beggar, passed by contemptuously at the roadside?

And though the greedy man is vilified by those who would elevate themselves to the high moral ground, they perceive through unseeing eyes, for in truth he is the unsung benefactor of mankind. For in the very act of taking and making his own, he is giving free expression to the blueprint of the human soul that was conceived before the beginning of time.

In this unforgiving world there is no place for altruism and generosity of spirit, except among those who would feign humbleness and seek to ingratiate themselves by false modesty and self-denial. He who would present himself as never seeking more than mere subsistence levels speaks with the spurious sincerity of a bookmaker paying out winning punters with a forced smile.

For no man on this planet is totally without greed – let no espouser of high ideals fool you into believing otherwise. From the moment of his birth, the young infant senses above all else his desire for the things of others and knows that he will not rest until he has acquired them. And as he seeks to grab the rattle from his baby brother's cot or wrest the cup of Ribena from the outstretched hand of his bawling nursery companion, he is unleashing the life-force that will sustain him through the trials of adulthood.

Thus he who would deny his greed is guilty of the worst

hypocrisy of all. Can the man driving a family saloon look you in the eye and say with total honesty that he has never beaten his fists on the bonnet and prayed to the Good Lord above for a Rolls Royce or a Ferrari that he can polish lovingly on his driveway and send his neighbours into paroxysms of envy? And the man who mortgages himself to the hilt to buy his dream home, does he not at the very moment of acquisition find his thoughts transporting him to the purchase of even better and bigger houses and mansions? And who is there amongst you who would really leave the last Ferrero Rocher chocolate for his fellow diners, when their hands are hovering with equal rapacity above the box?

In the age to come, when sentiment and self-denial have been exposed for the shallow impostors they are, men will come to recognise greed as a virtue. Greed makes macho men of wimps and lifts timid under-achievers to new thresholds of attainment. For it is in the knowing that greed offers up its ancient secret and rewards those who seek its power. And when men of little understanding seek to chastise you for your greed, rebuke them, saying, why would you not want more and more of something that is good? And how can something be intrinsically good unless you want more and more of it?

So as you seek a self-perpetuating greed that knows no limits, be as the mighty oak tree spreading its roots and the boorish commuter taking up two seats on the morning train. And when you truly begin to think with the mind of greed and covet all that is not yours, remember the innate hunger of man for that which he does not truly need. Carry with you this simple truth: the only reason a great many families do not own an elephant is that they have never been offered an elephant for 10% down and interest free credit.

Then an earnest young man with a haughty look, a phone in each hand and a personal organiser clutched beneath his arm, rose to his feet and answered an incoming call before saying: Speak to us, oh lord and master of the Square Mile and far beyond, speak to us of mobile phones.

And Piers responded, saying: The Cullinan Diamond in all its glory, the Mona Lisa in its enigmatic beauty, and the Taj Mahal in its transcendental splendour, each one of these is in its own way a wonder of this awe-inspiring world, yet none of those things come close to the magnificence of the mobile phone. Seminal inventions like wide-screen television, Play Station and the I-Pod, have elevated man to new levels of sensory experience, whilst substances like cocaine, alcohol and Viagra have lifted the human capacity for sensual gratification into the stratosphere. Yet as surely as the wild geese fly south in the winter, nothing has changed the core of man's being-in-the-world like the mobile phone.

For in its power-bestowing uniqueness the mobile phone has broken the shackles of wearisome landline dependency and delivered stunning new vistas of communication and personal liberty. And though Sartre has said that man is condemned to be free, the mobile phone has provided him with a freedom unprecedented in the annals of human experience. In the midst of chaos, confusion, impenetrable traffic jams and motorway madness, when the swirling mists of winter descend like burial shrouds across the moors, and when night falls in the city and the demons of base criminality stalk the backstreets intent on robbery, murder and mindless destruction, the mobile phone is the ultimate rescuer, opening instantaneous pathways to sanctuary.

And when those closest to you, old and young, undertake perilous journeys, ill-equipped to face the hazards of a world that grows more hostile and unpredictable every minute, consider the inner peace there is to be found in the knowledge that they carry with them the key to instant salvation, through the swift touch of a mobile phone. For just as a rapid intake of oxygen offers sweet relief to he who lies desperately ill, so the dulcet ring of a mobile can be the very breath of life itself.

Yet know you that the mobile's true strength is not to be found in the realm of personal communication, but in the cut and thrust of commerce, where the foolish man is permanently lost in a fog of indolence, and the wise man is ever on his guard against the insidious pull of complacency. For the great and good of the business world build their success on an unshakeable ability to remain one step ahead of the competition by staying in touch 24/7. For them, the mobile phone is as indispensable as the razor-edged teeth of the great white shark, or the uncanny night vision of the barn owl. Without the mobile link to keep them permanently connected to all four corners of the globe, businessmen and entrepreneurs would indeed be as ineffectual as toothless, sightless old men.

But beware, my bold fellow travellers in the new age of communication; take care, lest you lose yourselves in the seductive pull of the mobile's 'must have' public image. For though you would see your trendy flip-top phone as the epitome of style and coolness and carry it with you like a badge of post-modern technological awareness, the lure of worldly approval can render you blind to your own image as a wally of monstrous proportions.

For though you seek the admiration of those around you as you speak with clarity and confidence on the 7.25 to Waterloo, who is it who would willingly sit and listen over and over to the most depressingly evocative phrase of contemporary life: 'I'm on the train'? And who – were he not part of a captive audience – would have his ears assailed by the most mundane details of your private life and small talk so banal and mind-numbing that it would cause even a saintly man of God to wring his hands and curse in frustration?

In the hands of one who knows nothing of humility and self-restraint the mobile phone is nothing but a vulgar obscenity, but in the hands of a wise and temperate man it can access the beauty of creation itself. For when you are truly in tune with the higher calling of your mobile and experience its all-empowering touch, you will rise like a colossus through the limits of your consciousness and reach out to claim your rightful inheritance. Gaze into the keypad of your mobile and you will see the electronic code of life itself.

As Piers paused to take a sip of water, and a make-up girl leant across to wipe a bead of perspiration from his brow, an elderly woman, bedecked with diamonds and pearls that glinted like the morning sun, stood up and said: Princely and pre-eminent Piers, speak to us now of work.

And he began to speak with a vibrancy that came from the depths of his being, for the old woman had highlighted one of his favourite topics. Work is a gift from the heavens that should never be avoided, disparaged or taken lightly, he told them. For in your work is the expression of the divine, the mystic and the eternal, and in the way you go about your work can be seen the essence of your only true self. For just as the eyes are the windows to the soul, so is a man's work a living revelation of his innermost qualities and character.

Though conventional wisdom would tell you that all work and no play makes Jack a dull boy, do not heed this logic of fools. Work gives meaning to those who would otherwise be bereft of motivation and inspires those who are forever floundering in a sea of meaningless striving and seeking.

And though the masses seek escape from work through the lottery and other illusory roads to riches, in your heart you know the timeless truth: work sustains and revitalises the inner man. For you have only to observe those who view retirement as the Holy Grail of life to see the creeping paralysis of disillusionment and the incipient sting of death etched on their faces like a tombstone.

And though the term workaholic is seen as a criticism and a curse, see it rather as a blessing and a compliment. Far from making men dull, work renders them alive and proud and fulfilled and, most important of all, it lights the way to wealth, power and personal freedom. Who would consciously seek the fruitless lure of play, when he can have the life-enhancing pleasure of work? For in his mindless quest for shallow, directionless leisure, man is trapped by the empty dictates of a lost and misguided society.

Those who would pour scorn on young city whiz-kids working long and interminable days, see only through the distorted lens of one whose sight has been irretrievably dimmed. For what is it to take a lunch-hour but to engage in a pointless distraction from the only truly meaningful activity known to man? And what are weekends but frivolous and damaging interruptions to that same centrality of purpose? And what is home-life compared to the eternally sustaining power of joyfully-undertaken, health-enhancing work? And holidays, though not entirely devoid of merit for those who have already made their pile, are for the most part like needless pit stops to a Grand Prix driver on his way to glorious victory at Monza or Hockenheim.

And the wife who berates her husband for staying late at the office night after night, looks only with one-dimensional vision. For she is mindful only of her temporary deprivation and sees not that he is enriching their relationship with the fullness of life's potential, as well as loosing the yoke of financial oppression from their backs. And if in the course of his strivings he dallies fleetingly with his secretary in a meaningless liaison, so be it, for such are the indisputable needs of lusty men of commerce, and to deny them their harmless indulgences would be to shackle their creative spirit beyond redemption.

Work should be all things to all men, and those who trudge wearily towards the train station each morning, bemoaning their fate, clutching their briefcases with bitterness in their hearts, envying those who go about their business with the bright-eyed enthusiasm of a squirrel unearthing its nuts in springtime, cursing the day they sacrificed their souls on the corporate altar, have missed the point as comprehensively as the man who fails to see the beauty in a well-ordered balance sheet.

For though it is true that work – genuine work that sees profit as its only end – demands nothing less than utter single-mindedness and commitment, it is not by the sweat of your brow that you will truly make your mark as a man of vision and commercial supremacy. Always remember that the essence of work in its purest and most productive form is ninety per cent inspiration and ten per cent perspiration. Just as the pen will always defeat the sword, and the subtle manoeuvres of the martial arts expert will reduce the blundering aggression of the muscle-bound bully to frustrated impotence, so a brilliant and original – and a devious – mind will always outstrip a plodding workhorse.

And remember, too, that whilst play and relaxation are of themselves as worthless as a sliver of cut glass to a diamond merchant, your work should nevertheless be as a computer game to a young boy, or a Barbie doll to a little girl. Each and every moment of your working day should be imbued with pure passion, and your hunger for work should be as insatiable as the drug addict seeking his latest fix.

So as you pursue the daily dance of commercial striving and fill your personal organiser to overflowing with board meetings, corporate deals and international trading conferences, seek diligently to make your workplace your playground, your boardroom your gymnasium and your office your club room. And let your computer terminal be as a musical instrument pouring forth the music of life itself.

And before the final accounting comes, remember: he who labours without love for his work is like the art forger whose canvas reflects only the aura of the one whose skill imbued the original work with greatness, or the fawning servant whose very humanity is subjugated to his master's every whim. For why would you struggle the whole of your life at a job that does not excite and inspire you on a minute-by-minute basis?

Within the work ethic is enshrined the secret of inner harmony, and the man who seeks to belittle the things of work denies the calling of his noblest self. So be as the sequoia tree, spreading your roots wide and deep. Let your work pervade the totality of your knowing and let it wash over your every thought as honey dripping from the hive. And as you bask in the afterglow of work meticulously and joyfully completed, you will indeed know the reason for your being.

Then a bespectacled man, with wispy grey hair and a scholarly look, implored him: Speak to us now of words. And a mystical smile illuminated Piers' face and he answered, saying: Your words create your world. For just as in the Book of Genesis it is written that God created our world by speaking it into being, so everything you utter from your lips has real and lasting ramifications for your life.

For words have unseen, supernatural power, and what you say about yourself will come to pass as surely as the Grim Reaper stalks each and every one of us. So if you tell yourself you are a useless sack of animal droppings, with an IQ more fitting to a centipede, or if you speak unceasing negativity, convincing yourself that your life is destined for disaster in every department, you have written your life-script in indelible ink and the more you speak it, the more it will build on itself, and your future will be set in slabs of immovable concrete that oppress and disempower you.

But if you speak only positive and enabling words to impel yourself forward into each new day, your path to infinite success will be as inexorable as the rising of the sun. For words are like seeds growing inside you, and every verbal seed you plant will eventually bring forth fruit of one kind or another. And if you would desire only sweet-tasting fruit to enrich your life, be on your guard not to allow bitterness, self-loathing and recrimination to spew forth from your mouth, or your harvest will be as barren as a farmer's field after the monsoon.

For it is no secret that my extraordinary success is built, amongst other things, on a carefully instigated platform of self-affirmation. As I rise refreshed from my bed, acclaiming the dawn of each new day with joy and anticipation, it is as *de rigueur* for me to exhort myself with powerful, positive words as it is for a woman to apply her make-up, enabling me to reach out for unparalleled new levels of performance and achievement.

Just as a great sporting champion owes his success to his indomitable will to win and an attitude of mind that implicitly believes that he and he alone has the divine right to wear the gold medal round his neck, so I, in my daily act of self-assertion, refuse even to contemplate anything other than victory of the most complete and crushing kind; for my dictionary knows not such weasel words as defeat, surrender, compromise or, most contemptible of all, quit.

And when we have lived out our lives and await the great mystery of what lies on the other side of this mortal existence, then will we truly curse ourselves and rue the day we were born, if our words have led us to nothing but missed opportunity and under-achievement. Since, as John Whittier has written, for all sad words of tongue or pen, the saddest are these: It might have been!

Yet it is not merely in what we say about ourselves that we must guard our words. In our interactions with our fellow human beings, words must be weighed as carefully as precious stones by a jeweller. For, whilst words can charm and uplift and soothe like honey, they also have the power to wound and to crush.

And though children, and many adults too, have traditionally countered verbal assaults by saying sticks and stones may break my bones but names will never hurt me, is that not one of the most misleading and potentially dangerous misconceptions known to man? For, whilst physical attacks may harm the body, the damage caused by venomous and vile words can eat away at the recipient like an incurable disease.

Thus do spouses and lovers, with verbal barbs and cruel jests, erode and destroy the very fabric of their relationship. And so too do parents, by their unthinking and unfeeling criticism of their children, sow seeds of negativity and limitation, blocking their true potential and leaving them forever blighted by demons of self-doubt.

For words cling to the unconscious mind like limpets and become as much a part of a person as their physical being, shaping and conditioning them, freeing them to be whatever they would wish to be or condemning them forever to live in the pit of pessimism. And be under no illusion; to undo the cumulative effect of words is as impossible as prising open an oyster with bare hands. For the verbal template is imprinted on the victim's psyche, and to take away his long-held beliefs about himself, however distorted, would be to remove the very core of his identity.

So, at all times and in all situations, treat words with the utmost reverence and caution. Above all do not spew them out over-zealously or injudiciously as a woman of loose morals offering her favours. For, as Shakespeare has written, men of few words are the best men. Remember, when in doubt, zip the lip; for those who weigh their words and contain them do not wound thoughtlessly nor offer hollow praise. Nor do they give away the secrets that imbue them with their inner fire and strength, nor expose their weaknesses and foibles to those who would home in on them like vultures swooping on a carcass.

And though I stand before you now speaking out the truths that have contributed to my stature in the world of commerce, yet am I exercising the strictest care and judgement in the things I reveal to you. For, as it has been written, the tongue, though small and seemingly insignificant, is potentially powerful beyond measure, being in essence like the rudder of a ship with the ability to steer you on a course to triumph or disaster. And in the final reckoning, when the choice is to hold fast and remain silent or pour forth idle chatter, remember the truth of these age-old words: empty vessels make most noise.

Then a deeply tanned and elegant man, a former board member, who had been pensioned off with a golden handshake of outlandish proportions, rose to his feet and said: Oh, omniscient Piers, speak to us now of business.

And Piers, feeling the words flow from his innermost being, answered, saying: Though men of religion and academic wisdom will tell you differently, be not swayed by mindless sentimentality, for the world is built on business. Without the cut and thrust of commercial manoeuvring and the ceaseless hum of international trading, how would this cold and bellicose planet sustain itself? And without the ebb and flow of world markets, how could the all-providing infrastructure of healthy capitalism be maintained? And if the creative energy of businessmen ceased to burn brightly in their breasts, how would shareholders and those who invest their hard-earned savings and their pension funds in public companies reap the harvest of increased profitability?

The artist, as he gently strokes the canvas with his brush, breathes vibrant life into the unseen creation of his mind; the potter, as he turns his wheel, transmutes shapeless clay into a thing of lasting pleasure and beauty; the sculptor, as he wields his chisel with the subtle touch of a brain surgeon, hews raw stone into a delicate work that gladdens the soul.

So too the businessman, as he plots and schemes with tireless mental dexterity, does not merely accrue to himself the rewards of narrow self-interest. His striving and his acumen create a feeling of fellowship and corporate belonging for those who are mere hangers-on to his coat-tails. For does not the one who would cloak himself in the afterglow of sweet commercial victory allow those beneath him to bask in the reflected glory of his finest hour?

Yet know you that true success in business comes at a price. As the dove flies silently to its nest at nightfall, so the march of businessmen committed to unprecedented levels of turnover shall seek to transform this world of limited thinkers. But the old guard, those of pinstriped suits, old school ties and rolled up copies of *The Times*, will resist with all their might, condemning the new ways and advocating a return to more conservative days. There will be weeping and gnashing of teeth and even the most formidable and feted corporate wunderkinds will not be left unaffected.

For the new age of business is upon us, and woe betide he who is left behind in the stultifying mire of the old ways. As the mantle of e-commerce casts its spell, let no man be under any illusion. The businessman who sits at his computer and curses the day Bill Gates invented Microsoft will be as a wilting flower in the desert sun. The entrepreneur who fights against the tide of dotcom enterprise will be swept away like a tiny fishing boat in a hurricane. And he who buries his head in the mists of time, lauding the old ways of bartering and wheeler dealing, will find himself stranded helplessly like a floundering whale on the shore.

Therefore, be unceasing in your endeavours, and as cunning as the fox slinking through the wire of the chicken run whilst the farmer sleeps, blissfully unaware of the marauding presence in his own backyard. Know your enemies as you would yourself, for in the priceless knowledge of your adversaries and their *modus operandi* lies the key to your own inexorable progress. Stand alone but cultivate an unimpeachable network of loyal and trustworthy contacts, so that nothing that happens within the vast parameters of the business world stays unknown and unscrutinized.

Ceaselessly travel the highways and byways of fiscal plenitude and boldly go wherever men of commercial standing gather. Make it your goal to know every innuendo and whisper, so that the tasks that fall to you on the way to achieving the power and profit of your innermost dreams are as straightforward as a child's abacus to a professor of pure mathematics. For business is the alpha and omega of civilisation. And, as long as men tread this earth, the wheels of commerce will provide the quintessential motivation for human endeavour.

Go, dream your dreams of spiritual fulfilment; cast your eyes on the misty horizons of the psyche, chase like the wind after the lingering mysteries of the soul, but put your trust not in these transient manifestations of human understanding. If you would seek to gain entry into the pantheon of knowledge, put your trust in the ways of commerce and seek only the things of the boardroom and the trading floor. For in your business brain lies the key to eternal oneness, and in your corporate heart you will find the answers to the ultimate questions of our existence here on earth.

As Piers prided himself on his extraordinary wisdom and eloquence, which he knew came not from this world but from the very heavens themselves, a small bespectacled man in quaintly formal attire that seemed more suited to a bygone age rose to his feet and said: Oh great and gracious tsar of the economic stratosphere, speak to us now of accountants.

And Piers smiled, saying: I thank you, kind sir, from the depths of my being, for in offering me an opportunity to speak of this most caricatured and undervalued of all professions, you have given me licence to rectify one of the most insidious misconceptions of our age. The accountant, as he pursues his craft without flamboyance or ostentation, will always be the object of ignorant jest, yet it is in the immutable blandness of his ways that his true genius is to be found.

For the essence of greatness lies not in the things we see but in those things which transpire in the secret places where the glorious gifting of one's birthright is refined to shimmering perfection. Just as the Olympic athlete preparing for his moment of destiny hones himself on the training ground, driving his tortured body until the sweat trickling from his brow becomes a torrent of pain and self-denial, so the accountant working diligently and meticulously amidst the mountain of invoices, balance sheets and tax statements, paves the way for glory of a far more lasting and fulfilling kind.

Yet in his tireless push for the spoils of victory there is one vast difference between the champion of the numbers and the medal-seeking Olympian. It is, for the most part, not to build his own reputation that the accountant strives so zealously, but for the glorification of the captains and generals of commerce and industry. And if in his unsung endeavours he becomes indelibly anodyne and unappealing, a colourless, characterless man who exhibits all the charisma of a stale cheese sandwich, this is also part of his singular talent.

For in his all-pervading greyness the accountant cloaks himself in an aura of reliability and respectability. And, as such, he is, with a few notable exceptions, the last person to arouse suspicion or controversy. Thus can he become a buffer between the forces of uncompromising legality and retribution and the unfettered ambition of the thrusting man of commerce, who seeks to carry himself and his company to ever-greater financial horizons by any means his trusty man of figures can devise. For many a vast commercial empire and many a splendiferous boardroom career has been shaped on the innovative wheel of creative accounting.

As great artists like Rothko and Mondrian blended together an amorphous array of shapes and colours to create a visual feast on canvas, so the accountant weaves his financial magic with a concoction of tax loopholes, tax shelters, offshore bank accounts, write-downs and write-offs, to produce a tapestry of tax avoidance that is truly beautiful to behold. And if in his displays of fiscal eloquence he strays a little from the paths of financial regulation, who is to say that he is any worse than the politician who is economical with the truth or the lawyer whose spiralling fees are a travesty of true recompense?

Yet in your gratitude to the Svengalis of the balance sheets, be not swayed beyond reasoned objectivity. For the ethos of commercial supremacy is forged in the fires of self-advancement, and true self-sacrifice is as rare as a soft-hearted pawnbroker. So, whilst these self-effacing men are indeed unceasing in their labours for the benefit of those who employ them, there is for the accountant himself the potential for financial reward that can carry him to his own heights of opulence. And even though his persona may seem more suited to the faceless masses than the ranks of the movers and shakers, does not many an accountant boast an even more lavish and enviable lifestyle than those whose books he lovingly nurtures?

So know you that whilst in his outer trappings the accountant is the soul of anonymity, he is rarely what he seems. Show me a po-faced paper-pusher and I will show you a swaggering hero, a William Wallace of the boardroom, a Lancelot of the commercial battlefield, jousting fearlessly against the armies of the taxman and the VAT inspector. And though the world appears to pass him by as he sits single-mindedly at his desk, the epitome of soulless passivity, in his carefully-ordered strivings he is as deadly as the cobra, silent yet poised to strike with lethal swiftness. For the accountant, too, dreams mighty dreams of greatness; he, too, seeks to write his name large in letters of gold on the eternal balance sheet of the cosmos.

And though your mind seeks the vainglorious high of self-promotion, deep inside you yearn to be as he of the sober suit and boring tie, unseen but always seeing, impassive yet burning with inner passion, bereft of glamour and magnetism yet filled to overflowing with single-minded dynamism. For does not control of the yearly accounts and audits confer ultimate power on he who undertakes them? Does he not have the fate of even the most consummate master of corporate strategy in the palm of his hand, knowing that in his artful juggling of the company's books he can either lift his paymaster to unprecedented new levels of profit and approbation or plunge him into oblivion?

For it is beyond question that my team of unparalleled accounting artists, labouring ceaselessly to maximise my fortune and broaden my empire, have carried me to the highest peaks of commercial glory. Yet understand that it has not been without my own personal diligence and intervention into their secretive ways that I have come this far without more than the most superficial wounds. For the laudable sway of self-interest will eventually ensnare even the most incorruptible of men. And though he strives to produce yearly figures of the most glittering hue, how can it be that the accountant would resist the temptation to salt away unseen sums for himself?

Thus must you be as the night owl, seeing under cover of darkness, forever ensuring that these men of devilish cunning are under surveillance, stepping in boldly to clip their wings when they fly too high for their own good. For it is true that I have sacked more accountants than most public companies employ in a generation, and it is only in my unfailing magnanimity that I have sent them on their way with golden handshakes far beyond their merits.

Yet be not dismayed by my caveat, for in its true and pure form accountancy is a profession of the highest honour and reward. If you would spurn the high of self-aggrandisement and seek fulfilment of the unpretentious kind, be as the bass player in an orchestra or the mechanic in a Grand Prix team, going about your business unacclaimed and invisible, fashioning yourself into an irreplaceable cog in the commercial carousel. And when you have shuffled off the self-serving demands of the ego and assumed the mantle of all-pervading drabness, then will you become an indispensable grey blob on the corporate landscape, a John Major of the corridors of commercial power.

Then a pale and sickly looking man, dressed in a style more appropriate to a street trader, stood up and demanded: Tell us, oh suave and charismatic one, of honesty and fair dealing.

Piers pondered for a while and then he spoke, saying: In this dog-eat-dog world the ethical and the above board shall be your burial shroud, and the devious and the underhand shall carry you through to born-again business life. And though you state your word is your bond, mean it not at any price, for it shall pay you handsomely to lie through your teeth and to devise ever more undetectable ways of dodgy dealing, as the yoke of increasingly oppressive financial regulation begins to bite.

Set your course in the murky waters of behind-the-scenes financial kick-backs and seek your reward in the nether world of fat backhanders and insider trading. Look to the coffee houses and the bars where the dishonest brokers gather to dream rich men's dreams and to the cheap hotels where old men of commerce seek solace with their secretaries and unwittingly leave the secrets of the boardroom on the bedroom floor.

A fair and honest man will not be found wanting when the taxman comes to call; nor will he be dragged away kicking and screaming when the financial regulators stalk the corridors of power like avenging angels. But where will his fantasies of wealth be when the final reckoning is upon him? And how will he look his children in the eye and tell them that their father worked every hour God sent for a pay cheque that scarce kept the bailiffs from the door, when by a process of straightforward dishonesty he could have had countless blank cheques at his fingertips? And what will he tell his disillusioned wife as she walks scornfully out of the door to meet her rich new lover, knowing that his late nights at the office were not a lie but far worse – a squandering of precious time and opportunity that can never be regained?

For what is honesty but the immature self-righteousness of one who would seek to ingratiate himself with the world at any price? And what is fair dealing but the gutless surrender of one whose appetite for victory and ever greater ascendancy has been dissipated in a meaningless froth of self-denial. And who, in the last resort, is to say what is honest and fair? For what may seem a monstrous example of underhandedness in one man's eyes may appear justified and even praiseworthy to another.

Ask yourselves where the business world would be without power-crazed autocrats to cast aside spurious notions of fair play in the pursuit of ever greater profits for their companies? For is it not true that the self-serving ruthlessness displayed by men of such extraordinary vision stirs and arouses the masses and galvanizes them to protect their own interests?

Yet there is danger, too, within the nurturing bosom of deviousness. The child seeking to hide his misdeeds from his parents is preparing himself for the strictures of adulthood, but he must take care not to conceal the truth from himself. The pupil dreaming up ever more inventive reasons why he has not handed in his homework on time is igniting the creative fires that will light his way to innovative excellence in the thornier testing ground of the workplace, yet he must beware the creeping sickness of being unable to tell fantasy from reality.

You asked of honesty and fair dealing and you would doubtless have me extol these so-called virtues as the epitome of all that is noble. Yet who can truly say that in the furnace of big business he has made himself whiter than the holy man who contemplates life from the closeted vista of his cell and has never given in to his baser instincts? When opportunities arise to pursue the path of self-advancement, it is only a man of singular self-denial who can resist. And, in the end, will he reap just reward for his abstinence?

So tread trustworthy paths, if you must, and seek motivation in all that is straightforward and beyond reproach. But lose your capacity for double dealing and going back on your word, and you are as dead as the dodo. And remember, above all, the words of the first Stock Exchange soothsayer many long years ago, and carry them with you to your grave: honesty pays – but not enough.

And as a television camera moved in for a close-up, Piers straightened his tie and took another sip of water, smiling beneficently for the television audience. And as he did so, a beautiful young woman seated near the back stood hesitantly and said: Handsome and magnificent benefactor of so many legions of fortunate employees, speak to us now of clothes.

Fixing her with his gaze, he replied, saying: You are what you wear. For in the outer manifestation of the clothes that you present to the world can be seen the true expression of the inner man – and woman. Indeed, when we speak of the naked truth, should we not rather be saying the fully clothed truth? For the body without clothes is as an army without a flag to march under, or a football team without home and away strips.

And he who labels men and women of fashion as empty-headed popinjays and mindless bimbos knows not the subtle power and symbolism of carefully-chosen clothes. And those who dismiss innovative men of fashion as producers of worthless ephemera do not comprehend the underlying significance of their work. For in their efforts to embody the spirit of self-enhancement and bravura, designers like Armani and Yves Saint Laurent have accessed a seminal aspect of success. A fashion statement, diligently and expertly made, is as compelling and effective as a towering intellect or a rapier-like wit.

And those who spend vast sums on psychotherapy and counselling to ease their troubled minds have ignored the inherent healing value of clothes. For just as sunshine is the best and most instantly accessible form of therapy known to man, so clothes carefully chosen and worn with a specific purpose in mind can shore up flagging self-esteem, lift dark moods and elevate the wearer to new levels of well-being and confidence.

Yet remember that while power dressing has become a watchword for our age, it is not in aggressive posturing alone that your threads can turn heads. For in the seductive high fashion of women of elegance and good taste, and the understated machismo of sharply-dressed men, lies the capacity – in the words of that greatest of human motivators, Dale Carnegie – for winning friends and influencing people, in every walk of life and each and every situation.

And in your choosing be bold and imaginative as the rock star or the Hollywood actor, for whom flamboyance is as natural as nakedness to a newborn babe. For when a timid man cloaks himself in the apparel of a man of worldliness and authority, though initially he feels apprehensive and self-conscious, yet will he through osmosis become as the clothes themselves, feeling bold and confident and free from self-doubt as the empowering new image kicks in.

And though she may be seen as loose and wanton, a woman who delights in garments that highlight and reveal her femininity is merely complying with a basic tenet of nature. Those feminists who decry their more liberated sisters for portraying women as base objects of male desire choose to ignore one undeniable fact of life: a woman's ability to tease and cajole is a foundation stone of human relations. For did not nature endow us with the capacity to entrance and excite those with whom we would bond, in order that we should have the bliss of sexual union, and, ultimately, the drive to reproduce the species? And ask yourselves this: if love is blind, why is lingerie so popular?

Know you, therefore, that filling your wardrobes with rows upon rows of clothes and your cupboards with more pairs of shoes than Imelda Marcos is as much a part of being human as sexual desire, or imbibing hot soup on cold winter mornings. And even those who have reached a certain age and stand accused of being mutton dressed as lamb have a right to strut their stuff, however ridiculous and past their sell-by date they may appear in the eyes of a narrow-minded world. The wearing of clothes to make us feel good is our birthright and the true watchword of our time should indeed be, 'If you've got it flaunt it'. For if birds and animals can engage in the most ostentatious mating displays to lure the object of their desire, why should men and women not do likewise?

And whilst it is an absolute 'no no' for men and women of consequence to be seen in the same outfit twice at business meetings or social gatherings, do not treat your clothes as dispensable rags, to be worn once or twice and then discarded as a snake sheds his skin. Treat your wardrobe as a shrine and offer even your cheapest chain store clobber the respect and attention you would accord yourself, never leaving it to languish in the washing basket or on the bedroom floor like a teenager's putrid socks.

Yet in your drive to impress and win over those you would seek to influence and attract, be on your guard; he who uses clothes to maximum effect knows in his heart their limits. For it is a well-balanced combination of the inner and the outer that makes a man what he is and sets him apart him from his fellows.

And yes, it is true, I wear the finest Italian suits and silk ties that money can buy, and my shoes are hand-crafted in Jermyn Street. Yet in my heart I know that it is my personal charisma that underpins my immaculate appearance and thus my outward show of authority.

So scour the shops and boutiques and shop till you drop in pursuit of the ultimate in trendiness and sophistication. Dress to kill and undress to thrill but above all else remember – fashion can be bought but style you must possess.

Then a tall, distinguished man, highly esteemed in the financial sector, rose from his seat in the front row, saying: Oh great and fearless deliverer of everything that we undeserving and humble shareholders have dreamed of and more, at this most momentous of times for our company, speak to us of adversity.

And Piers responded with alacrity, saying: Adversity is the flame on which your inner steel is forged. Those whose lives have never been touched by catastrophe or have never felt the bitter sting of defeat know not the power of the ultimate motivational force. Nor do they have the resources to withstand the harsh and potentially backbreaking tests and trials of life when they come, as they inevitably will.

For suffering and loss are as much a part of our human existence as birth, marriage and death. And, as such, they are vital components of life. For, as Nietzsche has said, what does not kill me makes me strong. So the businessman who has never been at the point of calamity and desperation will be as a swaying reed in the wind when his adversaries seek to plunder and destroy that which he has painstakingly created. But he who has fought his way through a succession of bitter commercial battles will emerge as a finely tempered blade from the fire, honed and ready for anything the world can heap upon him.

Though you see me standing here as the epitome of success and worldly accomplishment, know you that it was not always this way. For, although my greatness was preordained, the place from whence I came was steeped in mediocrity and misery. And the road I travelled on, in my flight from dark despair, was frequently as debilitating as the march of a weary legionnaire in the heat of the desert sun. Yet through my ability to treat adversity as a friend I rose above the choking mundanity of my origins, so that it was but an inconsequential blip on the chart of my inexorable progress.

For it is in the heat of battle that courage hitherto unrecognised instinctively manifests itself. Just as great leaders emerge from the ranks of seemingly insignificant and ordinary men to stir their compatriots to rise up and break the yoke of tyranny and dictatorship, so the man of true commercial steel dismisses the ignominy of bankruptcy and is unmoved when his investments plummet, using what might seem like an insuperable crisis to those less blessed with resilience and the power of lateral thinking to lift himself to new and greater heights.

And though in his darkest hour, when the creditors close in and the bailiffs have taken away his art treasures and his wife's most expensive jewellery, he may be tempted fleetingly to leap from the window of his penthouse, or to reach for his finest antique duelling pistol to blast himself to oblivion, it is but a momentary lapse of reason for the man whose true valour is kindled in adversity. For at the very moment when his senses exhort him to shuffle off this mortal coil, the colossus that lies dormant inside him awakens from its slumber and galvanises him to assume the mantle of the man he was always destined to become.

Yet though many times you see the heroic and the ennobling happening before your eyes in circumstances that defy logic and belief, do you not convince yourself in your own times of despair that the gift of transforming defeat into glorious victory is for others, not for you? As the beaten and bloodied boxer throws in the towel, so you, in your acceptance of defeat as more than a passing stranger in your life, let in the creeping paralysis of uncertainty which, having found a foothold, spreads like a forest fire.

For mark this well: each of us has the capacity to overcome even the most vile and oppressive circumstances and rise up to become a leader, a visionary and a hero. So in your quest to banish all trace of negativity from your thinking, be as the great warrior, Robert the Bruce, who found inspiration in observing a spider rebuilding its broken web, time and again. Let surrender be a word that has no place in your dictionary. And though it is written in *Desiderata* that there will always be greater persons than you, heed not these self-defeating words.

And as you struggle against the forces that weaken your resolve, remember that nothing that appears initially to be harmful or debilitating is without a purpose. For it has been ordained that everything in this world has an opposite, and there is good reason for it to be so. For how could you enjoy the bliss of warm spring sunlight on your face if you did not also feel the depressing chill of dark winter evenings? And how could you know joy in all its fullness if anguish had never touched your sheltered life? And how could you savour the opulence of the Dorchester or the Waldorf if you had never spent the night in a cheap bed and breakfast at Southend-on-Sea?

Just as sickness spurs the seed of healing to germinate, and unknowing paves the way to enlightenment, so adversity will set the wheels of victory in train. And when you have reached out and grasped the helping hand of hardship, the accomplishment will be doubly sweet. And after you have fought your way through the fires of perfidious business dealing and emerged from the ashes of liquidation as a vibrant new man of serious commercial import, then will you bestride the Square Mile and make Murdoch and Branson seem like messenger boys fighting to gain a toehold on the corporate ladder.

And as heads all around the great hall nodded in silent affirmation, a dark bejewelled woman with the look of a high-class courtesan, stood to applaud him. Then she spoke, saying: Oh handsome and desirable Adonis of our prepotent corporate body, speak to us now of sex.

His eyes drank in her primitive beauty and he answered her, saying: You would have me talk to you of sex, but in truth you would be better served if I told you of making love. For to indulge in sex, pure and simple, is as straightforward and undemanding as microwaving a ready meal, but to make love requires the maturity and *savoir faire* of a gourmet.

Sex is the great seducer of our time, the narcotic of the people that promises so much and so often delivers emptiness and disappointment. For what is sex in its modern-day mindlessness but an addiction and, as with any addiction, the obsessive pursuit of sex promises to open the gateway to freedom and pleasure unlimited. Yet in its relentless pursuit of personal satisfaction and affirmation it offers only enslavement.

And though Alex Comfort's much-lauded book, *The Joy of Sex*, altered forever the way we view this fundamental human function, those four little words of that seminal title were a lie. For how many in our neurotic generation now find genuine joy in their sexual liaisons, seeing them rather as a kind of Olympics of the body, where ecstasy and bliss are subjugated to scrutiny and performance.

The myth of instant sexual bliss, as promulgated in countless glossy magazines and television programmes, is as insidious as it is false. For sex is driven by the mind far more than the body, and forever seeking to attain levels of sexual performance and fulfilment, as laid down by so-called sexperts of the media and Viagra-fuelled fantasy chasers like Peter Stringfellow and Hugh Hefner, can only lead to disenchantment and morbid introspection that is the very antithesis of what joyful sex should be.

For when two people come together in sexual harmony it should indeed be with the unbridled passion of wild horses galloping on the plains or the power of a tornado sweeping aside everything in its path. Yet it should also be as the waves gently lapping on the Caribbean shore or dawn breaking over the Serengeti. For sex is not merely the physical outpouring of pent-up libido; it is also the freedom cry of the human spirit tearing itself from the shackles of everyday tedium and rising up to the eternal pathways of the heavens.

And though the white heat of unfettered sexuality can open the door to new levels of ecstasy, so often it is the gateway to hell. For while it is true that I stand here before you as one who has tasted the manifold fruits of sexual pleasure in all its variety, enticing into my antique four-poster bed a succession of beautiful women that has made me the envy of many a Hollywood film star, yet is the fire of my innermost longing still unquenched, for I have found nothing but the briefest and most hollow satisfaction in those transient liaisons.

To know that women want me only for my perfect body and love-making skills that are truly a gift from the gods, has become nothing more than a tiresome irritation that renders those fleeting connections a meaningless travesty of interaction, forfeiting precious time that could have been infinitely better spent on coupling of the corporate kind.

For as any sex therapist worth her Masters and Johnson will tell you, the relentless pursuit of sexual gratification is a manifestation of a far deeper psychological need; a blindness far more incapacitating than any physical loss of sight, rendering the hapless victim incapable of seeing beyond the next peak of sexual ecstasy. Was it not that greatest of wordsmiths, Ernest Hemingway, who said, to be freed from the tyranny of sexual craving is like being unchained from a wild beast?

Yet know you that my intention is not to deny you the basic instinct that is your birthright. For sexual pleasure has its place in the eternal scheme of things and in its purest form it can lift a man to the portals of heaven. Thus he who has tasted not the joy of multi-orgasmic rapture is like a mountaineer who has never risen beyond the foothills of a great mountain range, or a gourmet who is condemned forever to consume the culinary travesties of Macdonalds or Burger King.

And if you would access the pathway to genuine sexual fulfilment, be at pains to cultivate those two most vital senses – a sense of humour and a sense of perspective. He who enters the bedroom with an unsmiling face, a suitcase full of sex toys and a grim determination to make the earth move for his partner to 9.9 on the Richter Scale will leave as bereft as a bride jilted at the altar. For an attitude of unyielding intensity and athleticism is the burial shroud of free-spirited sexuality.

Yet whilst viewing creativity and spontaneity as the keys to sexual bliss, take care not to douse those very things that kindle the flame of passion. To function as nature intended, sex must be treated with respect and prepared for with the thoroughness of a master chef planning the menu for a great banquet. For as with everything in the sphere of human endeavour, sexual fulfilment is not a matter of trusting to fortune but rather working ceaselessly to ensure the optimum conditions for success.

Thus, if you seek to consummate your longing in the frozen depths of mid-winter on the backseat of an ancient and weather-beaten Transit van, do not be surprised if desire melts away as swiftly as a sliver of Haagen-Dazs in the bosom of your beloved. And if you have cut corners in the shower, cut back on the deodorant and cut down on the after-shave, do not wonder why your partner recoils from your advances as they would if hit upon by a love-crazed orang-utan.

Be aware, too, that whilst I have warned you of the perils of an obsessive preoccupation with rumpy pumpy, there is, for those whose spirit yearns for the excitement of fleshly encounters of the most meaningless kind, a different level of fulfilment. For has not the groupie adding another rock star to her list made her star-struck sisters tear their tinted hair with envy? And the philanderer carving another notch in his bedpost – is it not true that the energy driving him on is a drug that many a hen-pecked husband would gladly have coursing through his own veins, to free him from the apron strings of stale domesticity?

So seek sexual gratification in all its fullness in the bedroom and the boardroom and in any situation where opportunity rears its seductive head. Bonk till you conk and perform great feats between the sheets, but remember above all else that it is in his metaphorical nakedness that a man can lose himself, for when passion is spent the true reckoning comes.

Then a thin and angular man, with an aura of authority and

affluence about him, rose to his feet and said: Speak to us now, oh phenomenon of the fiscal universe, speak to us of money.

And Piers smiled, saying: The only surprise in what you ask me is that the subject you would have me speak upon was not the first request made to me on this momentous day. For money is the essence, the lifeblood, the *sine qua non* of everything worthwhile that you see, everything you touch and everything you covet and desire. Money is your friend, your lover, your lifelong companion, your teacher, your counsellor, your mentor, your guide, your protector and so much more.

And though it has been said that money cannot buy friendship or love, this is twisted thinking at its most illogical and deceptive. For whilst it is true that there are those who would gravitate towards wealthy men purely for the size and purchasing power of their bank accounts, is it still not better to be rich than to swallow the bitter pill of immutable poverty?

The man who struggles through life, barely able to feed himself and his family and to pay for even his most basic necessities, is oftentimes so ground down by the daily battle to survive and so resentful of the hand that fate has dealt him that he finds it hard to reach out and give love and friendship in a way that is anything but superficial.

By contrast, the wealthy man is as a cormorant soaring free on the summer breeze, seeing everything far below him from the vantage point of one who has accessed freedom at its highest point, for he has the joy of knowing that he will never be in thrall to financial hardship and lacks nothing in any way, be it material or spiritual. Thus is he at liberty to use the power, position and personal characteristics that his money brings to attract and influence those he would seek to win as friends, lovers and associates.

And why would anyone not prefer the company of he who spends lavishly and is able to surmount the obstacles that frequently block the way of those less well-endowed financially? And though, as I have said, the cynics would point to self-interest and the promise of reflected glory as the motivation of those who seek out men of money, be not swayed by such talk for it is the bitter fruit of jealousy and small-mindedness and speaks far more damningly of he who makes the accusations than he who is the object of such vitriol.

The wealthy man thinks on a different plane, seeing everything in far-reaching, global terms. Thus, in his empire-building and his drive for ever-greater profits, is he able to provide work and opportunities for those less blessed with financial vision. And know you that capitalism is not the disempowering curse of ordinary men that Marx labelled it; rather it is a heaven-sent mechanism for the advancement of the individual and the community.

And though it has been written that the love of money is the root of all evil, how can that which sustains and provides, and offers joy and opportunity and freedom, as well as the ability to clothe and feed your children, and to buy the best medical attention for the sick, be called anything but good? And has it not also been said that a fool is someone who knows the price of everything and the value of nothing? Yet how could a man go through life unaware of the price of those things he needs and those he desires? For value is as subjective as a love of art or music, but a price tag represents the one true starting point for meaningful negotiation.

And whilst it will be seen by some as the ultimate in meaningless clichés, money does talk and does indeed make the world go round, being all things to all people and making all things possible, even those things which seem tantalisingly beyond reach. And in your longing for the all-encompassing power of money you would seek instant access to riches through the lottery, football pools and the gaming tables. Yet must you lay aside all thoughts of these demonic *divertissements*, eschewing the things of chance and pursuing instead the path of vision and inspiration – and in the initial stages, hard work and self-deprivation – and seeking ever-increasing profits by cultivating cunning and devious methods of business practice.

For those who have found disillusionment and emptiness in winning vast sums or securing overnight fame and fortune have failed to grasp the life-changing capability of money in its purest sense. Using windfall money merely to purchase bigger and more pretentious cars, mansions, gold necklaces and identity bracelets as thick as anchor chains will provide only temporary satisfaction for the hungry soul. And whilst these baubles are to be fleetingly enjoyed, it is in the astute management of money to build on itself and ensure financial impregnability that the quintessential value of money is realised.

Thus keep a goodly supply of cash around you at all times so you can hold it and caress it and look upon it with awe at every possible opportunity. Care for it as a gardener nurtures his plants, and speak to it as a love-struck Romeo whispers silken words to his Juliet. Then will your money blossom and grow as a child thrives under the tender ministrations of loving parents. For those who literally give praise to money's sovereign power as they worship the omnipotent greenback in America's Church of the Dollar have indeed discovered the master-key to life.

Yet be aware that not everyone who seeks after wealth is destined to grasp the spoils of financial victory. Just as a habitual choker on the edge of his greatest sporting victory hesitates at the very moment when he should be grinding his beaten opponent into the dust, so those who stand poised to acquire wealth beyond their dreams shrink like wilting flowers in the sun as they are confronted with the full magnitude of their achievement. And even amongst those who realise long-held dreams of wealth, there is frequently self-doubt and disillusionment as the unfamiliar persona of opulence disturbs the balance of their mind.

Yet is this self-denial not a monstrous sham? For he who denies his love of money, or his desire for a monster pay cheque and an ever-swelling bank account, is as guilty of hypocrisy as the religious man who preaches self-restraint whilst leaping between the sheets with his neighbour's wife.

And in the final accounting, is not the way of the world exactly as The Beatles, in their soulful Scouse simplicity, so eloquently described it? *The best things in life are free but you can keep them for the birds and bees. Now give me money.* And when they sang, *Money don't get everything it's true but what it don't get I can't use* and *Your lovin' gives me a thrill but your lovin' don't pay my bills,* were they not expounding a greater truth than any guru or prophet has ever done?

So flash the cash and smile at your pile at all times; put money as your goal above all else, relegating even those foundation stones of our society, morality, religion and the law, to a place of fitting subordination. And when you have deified money, immersed yourself in its life-changing possibilities and made it your one true reason for living, then will you feel yourself drawing near to paradise itself.

Then a young man in jeans and dark glasses, with the look of a rock star about him, stood up and implored him: Oh, stylish and charismatic leader of this lean and hungry generation, speak to us now of cars.

And he answered saying: The seductive power of a car lies not beneath the bonnet but within the deep and complex psyche of its owner. For it is not the speed of the car but the potential for living in the fast lane that spurs you to seek better and ever more ostentatious cars, so those you seek to impress would know you as one of exceptional taste and individuality.

A car can be all things to a man, from the purely functional to the sublime; and in the womb-like security of the driver's seat he can assume the mantle of a bold new identity with which he can take on the world with pride and confidence. For in the style and substance of a car lie the hopes and fantasies of men of all nations, social classes and religious denominations. Thus is your car your home, your office, your fortress, your playground, your badge of authenticity, and so much more besides.

And those who seek instant charisma and status behind the wheel of a Ferrari, a Porsche or an Aston Martin have indeed accessed the secret of personal magnetism. For in their throbbing power lies an outer manifestation of the inner man that speaks more of the unquenchable fire in his belly than a friend or marriage partner ever could. And those who denigrate these sleek machines as ephemeral symbols of wealth and ostentation speak only through veils of envy.

For just as the master swordsman with a duelling pistol in his hand is nothing but a toiling artisan, so a man who drives a car that does not stir his senses and spark the romance in his soul is suppressing the tiger in his tank as surely as if he were to deny his manhood. But know you that it is not only within the leather-clad interior of the most powerful and exclusive driving machines that a man's true essence can take flight. For inspiration is as individual as a fingerprint, and what is anathema to one man is ecstasy to another.

So if it is within the drab and unsophisticated interior of a Morris Minor or the salesman-like slickness of a Ford Mondeo that you find access to the dormant poet within, or awaken inside yourself the hero of your unspoken fantasies, then treasure that car as you would a necklace of diamonds and rubies, and do not be tempted by the fleeting lure of the showroom window and a more upmarket model that offers nothing but sleek bodywork and a towering reputation.

For a man and his car should be matched as perfectly as lovers luxuriating in the surrender of the first flush of passion. And as you and your car become one, so will you rise above the pedestrian limits of your conscious mind. In this blissful union with your automotive alter ego you will become all-seeing and comprehending, as the eastern mystic whose vision takes him far beyond the confines of this tawdry world.

For a car to a man of feeble imagination and limited thinking is but a necessary evil, a frustrating, costly means of travel, an atmospheric pollutant, another stress factor in an already pressured life. But to a man of vision and insight, a car is so much more than the sum of its meticulously engineered parts. It is a vehicle for transporting him to new heights of personal approbation, a persona that lifts him to levels of sensory satisfaction to which his mundane self can never aspire, and a babe magnet infinitely more effective than the most costly after-shave or a rippling six pack.

Yet whilst revelling in the freedom and charisma of your chosen automobile, take care not to undervalue it as a simple means of conveyance. For in this friendless, bellicose world, who in his right mind would choose to stand frozen and frustrated at bus stops, or suffer the indignity of cattle-like confinement on the underground, when he could be cosseted within the interior of his car, oblivious to the cacophony and the mayhem around him, whilst personalised music from his CD player caresses his ears and intimate conversation on his hands-free set soothes his inner man even in the most dire traffic jams?

So lavish affection on your car. Treat it as carefully as you would your own body, and it will reward you with the loyal service of a faithful manservant. Customise your car with technological wizardry, gadgets and personalised number plates, so it is an extension of your own true self. But in your enthusiasm be alive to the danger of lowering your image to one of vain posturing or vulgar ostentation. Do not rev your engine noisily at traffic lights in empty displays of machismo, or dangle furry dice from your driving mirror, or carry lurid signs like 'Wayne and Tracey' across your windscreen. For those who send out tacky messages of laddish connotation will receive nothing but derision and contempt.

Be aware, too, that just as surely as a lover's infatuation wanes over time, so a man's devotion to his chosen vehicle can disappear like the dawn mist. So as lovers parting with sweet sorrow, be alert and recognise that seminal moment when you and your car must follow different paths. For to stay chained to a car when the passion has ebbed away will drag you to the depths of despair. But to ease yourself into the driving seat of a new and more exciting model is to rediscover the explosive fire of creation itself.

And remember, as with all things you so fervently desire, that restraint is the key to maximising pleasure. It has been rightly said that it takes eight thousand, four hundred and sixty bolts to assemble an automobile and one nut to scatter it all over the road. And in this age of rampant road rage, is it not also true that anyone driving slower than you is an idiot and anyone driving faster is a maniac? Thus he who treats every street and motorway like a Grand Prix circuit has the brain of a spider monkey, for in his selfishness he cares nothing for those innocents he cuts up or runs off the highway.

And when you have found the wheels of your dreams, consider this: the best safety device is not anti-lock brakes or air bags but a rear-view mirror with a traffic cop in it. As a man drives, so shall he reap, and only when his car has become as a prayer book to a holy man, and not a lethal weapon in his hands, will he steer a course to true fulfilment.

And as Piers surveyed the awestruck audience hanging on every priceless pearl that came forth from his lips, he felt a sense of inner peace washing over him. And as he took another sip of water he heard a voice as gentle as the fluttering of angels' wings wafting towards him from the back of the hall. Even from a distance he could see clearly the ethereal beauty of the young woman who had begun to speak his name. Her words flowed sweetly, and he made a mental note to find her after the meeting and gladden her heart by offering her a few brief but meaningful moments of his precious time. And she begged him: Oh insightful and omniscient master of our great commercial universe, teach us now the timeless secrets of love.

Then Piers spoke, saying: Love is the great pretender. It arrives like the gentle spring rain, with the promise of eternal bliss, and leaves with the blackness of a funeral cortege. If I could offer you but one caveat above all else in this shallow and impermanent world, I would beseech you to beware the treachery of love. For in its cruel deceit love becomes as the most powerful anaesthetic to the consciousness of mankind, sending the human spirit soaring on gossamer wings before bringing it brutally to earth like a game bird fatally wounded by the poacher.

Love brings paralysing confusion to those whose purpose and

direction was as unshakeable as a mountain, makes weaklings of men of pride and status, and blinds those with even the most singular vision to everything but the seeming wonder of the object of their passion. Love is as the most powerful hallucinogenic drug that warps the mind, lures good and faithful men to rack and ruin, and drags them to the depths of misery and self-loathing.

And though poets and writers through the ages have spoken of love with coruscating words, filling thousands upon thousands of pages with the most eloquent and heartfelt eulogies, their outpourings are as pigswill to the palate. For it was Tennyson alone amongst the myriad of wordsmiths who saw this charade in its true fiendishness when he wrote, and most of all would I flee from the cruel madness of love.

Karl Marx famously averred that religion is the opium of the people, but he was surely culpable of one of the greatest untruths in history. For whilst it is true that the power-based dogma of religious ritual does indeed constitute an insidious and divisive form of brainwashing for the masses, did not Marx totally underestimate the narcotic power of love in its universal seductiveness?

Thus do you crave the high of a romantic union that excites and soothes the troubled mind. And as the two of you become as one, the heady scent of intimacy sends your senses surging like a young bird taking flight for the first time. And when passion peaks it does indeed seem, for a few fleeting moments, as if all the pain and disappointment of this harsh world is brought to nought. Yet know you that it is in the temporary numbing of the anguish and the loneliness that the real hurt lies.

For when the passion wanes and the loving words have all been spoken, all that is left is an empty shell, a travesty of meaningful human interaction, like a house built of bricks with no cement to bind them or a loaf of bread with no yeast to make it rise. As one bloody kill does not sustain the lioness and her brood longer than it takes for their appetites to revive, so the bliss and oneness which accompanies the initial stirring of the senses cannot maintain a relationship weighed down by the transience of human interaction.

And when people talk of a love-match made in heaven, even then will the desire and the longing be stilled as inevitably as the human body ultimately returns to dust. For, as it has been written, men are indeed from Mars and women from Venus, and those who would seek to bridge this astronomical divide are as foolish and unseeing as he who seeks his future in a crystal ball.

So at the very moment of your greatest longing I would urge you to hold back and look around you at the monstrous web, like that of the Black Widow spider, in which mankind is entrapped. Consider the multiplicity of books, songs, films and plays based solely on the notion of love, all-conquering and everlasting, and contrast this rank deception with the pain of broken relationships and the suicidal despair of spurned lovers. Then will you surely see the lie that has been perpetuated in the name of the most dastardly four-letter word a man can utter.

For how can anyone of true vision and understanding fail to see the potential nightmare that lurks within the obsessive focus on the ecstasy of wedded bliss? Is there anything in any field of human activity more calculated to disappoint than the life-changing hope which springs from that most hallowed day when hands are joined in a meaningless show of union and vows are so emptily given and sealed with the phoney symbolism of tiny bands of gold?

And how much hurt and misery has been inflicted in the name of love by those who would deceive and control in order to make themselves feel stronger and more secure, and those who cheat and lie and rob the besotted object of their spurious love of every last vestige of dignity and self-esteem?

Yet in all I have told you, dear brothers and sisters, be not blinded to the sublime possibilities of love in its most noble form. For is there anything more admirable in this world than the unconditional love of a mother for her child, an attachment and a caring so strong that she would willingly lay down her life for the infant she has nurtured with such unstinting devotion? And what of those men and women throughout history who have given their own lives so that others might live? Can such heroic selflessness be measured in mere mortal terms? Does not such complete abnegation of self testify to the ineffable transcendence of the human spirit?

Yet if you would ask me for the secret of love in its purest and most potent form, I would tell you, as with so many of these matters on which you have sought my infinite wisdom, to look inside yourselves. For I know, from the experience of a life that is the apotheosis of personal and professional satisfaction, that the greatest love of all is self-love.

And if they accuse me of arrogance and narcissism, I say who better is there to lavish your love upon than the only one in this world you can trust to put your interests first one hundred per cent of the time? For whilst narcissism is a foolish and misguided infatuation with oneself, my own self-love is indeed the real thing.

And when you have felt the silken caresses of this supernatural kind of love that knows no limits, has no truck with the treacherous utterances of shallow romanticism and carries no agenda other than pure self-advancement, then and then alone will your heart justly sing to yourself the words of Barry White, the splendiferous Walrus of Love: *You're the first, the last, my everything.*

Then a florid-faced man of flowing hair and Bohemian dress beseeched him: Magnificent and magnanimous master of all you gaze upon, speak to us now of friendship.

And he answered, saying: It has been written that no man is an island, yet in truth he should strive to be that very thing. For what is friendship but to lose oneself in base surrender to another and open oneself to the bitter pill of intimacy that must end with precious few exceptions in disillusionment and betrayal? You would seek the outstretched hand of friendship as a touchstone of human relations at their most fulfilling, yet the very thing you covet is that which can demean and destroy you.

And though the sagacious Francis Bacon wrote, the worst solitude is to be destitute of sincere friendship, do not let such pathetic words taint your mind. In your fear of isolation you strive to surround yourself with those who would fill your life with companionship and laughter, support you and compliment you, and those who would rush to your side when your own need seems greater than theirs. Yet consider a while the motivation for this seeming magnanimity and know that nothing in this world is without a price.

For in the very act of giving of themselves will they not debit your account with the most burdensome expectations? And whilst it is true that some ask nothing concrete in return, even they unconsciously seek nothing less than recognition and recompense for their sacrifice. And if you truly examine your own grounds for close encounters of the interpersonal kind, are you not also proffering friendship for nothing less than your own personal gain and satisfaction?

Thus is the yoke of friendship imbued with selfish longing, irrational emotion, demand and counter-demand, and so becomes a union of the most dependent and dangerous kind. And though you would profess to seek only that which is for the highest good of the other, subconscious stirrings of envy and resentment bare their teeth like a wild dog, transmuting the bond of friendship so it becomes little more than bondage.

It has been said that a friend in need is a friend indeed, but have there ever been words less filled with truth and sincerity? A friend who comes with neediness and supplication will drain the life-force from you as a vampire bat sucks the blood from its victim. For once the giving starts there is no knowing where it will lead, and what began as a simple act of human kindness can spiral into a parasitic ensnarement that leaves the giver feeling empty and used like a lover heartlessly dumped.

Know you, too, that the one who offers the hand of friendship in business is the most dangerous kind, a slippery viper whose carefully cultivated ways can charm and inveigle like the adulterous wife whose smile belies the faithless devil in her soul. Behind the carefully manicured exterior lurks a monster of machination, beguiling you into an alliance, then striking when your guard is down to bring you to your knees.

And in being an island, standing proud and alone, are you not securing for yourself the ultimate form of personal security, a wall of impregnability that closes you off to any possibility of treachery and betrayal? And though it has been said that a problem shared is a problem halved, those who have espoused that spurious philosophy have discovered, to their cost, the implications of opening oneself up to another, giving away one's priceless inner secrets and becoming as exposed and vulnerable as a lobster without a shell.

For what is the fear of being alone but a baseless reluctance to face the inner demons that plague the soul? Thus, as in all things, let courage be your watchword. In looking deep inside yourself and examining the unknowing motivation that leads you repeatedly to act against your own best interests, you will expunge the terror that binds and blinds you and find the very strength you seek so illogically in empty comradeship. For you alone have access to your most treasured longings, and you alone can manifest your destiny.

So what has been set apart let no man join together. Be as the hermit or the religious ascetic, replete with the joy of self-knowledge and true understanding of the eternal ways. Strive unceasingly to retain your independence; be not swayed by the words of ingratiating fools sheltering in the life-giving nurture of your shadow, and be forever vigilant against the deadly sway of those who would seek to rob you of your state of splendid isolation. For in your solitude lies the key to eternal knowing, and in standing alone and utterly self-sufficient you will surely become the coolest dude on the planet.

And as Piers felt himself growing ever more confident and elevated in stature, as he basked in the glare of the spotlight, a tall, distinguished man, who he knew as a fierce but perennially defeated adversary of old, rose to his feet and said with a voice heavy with irony: Oh rapacious controller of our commercial destiny, grace us now with your unparalleled wisdom. Speak to us of takeovers.

So, he told them, you would have me speak to you of takeovers at last. I knew this moment would come as surely as my words to you will make front page headlines in tomorrow's national newspapers. And yet again must I tell you that the secret you seek to prise from me can only be found by pursuing the thorny path of self-knowledge. For does not the sparrowhawk, as he twists and turns in pursuit of his prey, call forth the raw instinct of his inner being to make the final kill?

You would look to me as the perpetrator of your most unconscionable desires, projecting your own voracious appetites for corporate blood-letting onto my higher-profile persona so that you can deny the bellicose instincts that lurk beneath your benign exteriors. Yet as men of business, whose motivation can only be ever greater power and profit, why would you not acknowledge the swaggering conqueror that lies inside? And why would you seek to repress the lust for status and glory that courses through your veins?

For it is only in accepting the baser characteristics of your shadow side that you can truly know yourself and take hold of the life that was preordained for you. And it is only in allowing yourself to act out the darkest fantasies of your unconscious dreaming that you will access the warrior in your soul.

And as you tear the corporate flesh from your rivals, like a piranha stripping its hapless victim to the bone, and hear the anguished cries of those casualties of commercial war-mongering tossed aside like helpless bystanders, consider for one moment the true scenario which engulfs these passive bit-part players in a drama that is as old as commerce and money itself, and see the ultimate favour you bestow on them. For in casting them onto the streets with nothing but their laptop and their P45, are you not acting as an unheralded benefactor by causing them to search inside themselves for the untapped resources that through indolence and complacency have, for so long, remained dormant?

For there is indeed truth in the oldest of clichés, when one door closes another opens. Yet so often it is that which stares you in the face that proves the hardest of all to grasp, and in reaching inside yourself to find the courage to go through that open door, you hold back like a young gazelle hesitating at the edge of the chasm.

And to you who would suffer debilitating pangs of conscience as you lift the pen to sign the death warrant that will signal the demise of impotent corporate victims, the message is unequivocally clear: he who hesitates at the gates of Hades is lost, and he who is moved by wailing and gnashing of teeth as the helpless and the dispossessed plunge headlong into the abyss has not the inner steel to be a man of destiny. For such a man must have ice-water flowing in his veins and must manifest the detachment of a gunfighter cutting down his adversary without a scintilla of remorse.

Understand, too, that it is the swift and unyielding execution of the business coup that is the kindest cut of all. For why would you suffer a lingering death, racked with pain and soul-searching, when instant oblivion reaches out its welcoming hand? And is there not an unimpeachable dignity and nobility in ceding everything to one whose vision and genius is greater and more far-reaching than yours?

Know you that whilst a company is not greater than the sum of its employees, no individual is more important than the corporate good. The tide of expansion is as inexorable as the waves that sweep in from the ocean, and if anyone seeks to hold back the flow of energy that creates new leviathans of commercial endeavour, is he not attempting to pervert the course of history itself? So, strive not to be a martyr on the altar of business evolution. And do not resist the inevitability of the takeover, but look rather to a commercial makeover where you can rise again to new horizons of self-advancement and wealth.

For you have only to look at the eternal functioning of nature to see that the demise of one ensures the survival of another. Thus does the natural world maintain its glorious cycle of life and plenitude and ensure that those who follow us will indeed drink of the life-giving waters of universal renewal.

So whilst you may be tossed about in the maelstrom of hype and propaganda, never lose sight of the bigger picture that is being played out inexorably before your eyes. Free your mind from the constraints of small thinking, cast off the shackles of conscience and take on the mantle of the cold-hearted conqueror. When men say that the softest thing about you is your teeth, then will you be ready to join the movers and shakers of history.

And as Piers surveyed the rapt faces hanging on his every utterance, he felt a growing restlessness and reminded himself of the real reason why he stood there, feted and fawned over like a demigod. The hour has come when the talk must cease and the annexation of my most astute and dangerous corporate rival made a spectacular reality, he told himself. Though those who revere me and worship the ground I place my Gucci loafers upon would doubtless hear me dispensing my extraordinary wisdom into the night, I sense the clarion call of destiny at my shoulder, and I know that I must not wait a second longer to translate the rich but ultimately vain promise of words into swift and meaningful action.

And though those who I see lost in adulation before me will be left with the bitter sting of disappointment as I bring the flow of sagacity to a premature end, is it not true that they have been given more than enough for their workaday intellects to ingest? For it is indeed true that one can have too much of a good thing, and a surfeit of the profundity which I have heaped upon them would only leave them bewildered and uncomprehending.

Yet is it not better to have tasted the fruits of a great teacher in small measure than never to have tasted them at all? And is it not infinitely more edifying to have sat at the feet of the master for even one precious moment than to have passed many long years in the presence of a dozen men of inferior vision and understanding?

So whilst I will allow them to remain only partially filled and clamouring for more, yet will I set before them a dish of such coruscating wonder that they will forget their deprivation and become transfixed by the prize that I will place within their grasp. For as I have been at such great pains to inform them in my seminal discourse on takeovers, he who hesitates before he makes the final history-making putsch leaves the door ajar for his enemies and will reap the consequences as surely as the stock market rises and falls on a daily basis.

Cometh the hour, cometh the man, and, besides my own elevation to the business pantheon, is this not also the defining moment for those who would place complete and utter faith in my unparalleled track record? For here I stand, on the cusp of history, ready to lead them to the greatest corporate victory in the annals of western civilization. Now, at last, will I allow the world to see the magnitude of my commercial acumen, a spirit of acquisitiveness and empire-building so awe-inspiring that those who even attempt to confront it must beware, for, just like those who gazed upon the Medusa, they are in danger of being turned to blocks of stone.

Thus emboldened by his self-affirmations, Piers faced the meeting and prepared to speak to them again, pacing the podium with the swagger of one who instinctively knows he has been chosen to reside at the epicentre of greatness. And, sensing the mood and the time was right, he began to address them with the utmost confidence and inspiration.

Ladies and gentlemen, fellow shareholders in this most magnificent and incomparable corporation, you have been partaking of my singular wisdom for some while, and I, for my part, have been content in my magnanimity to open my heart and to share with you some of the foundational thoughts and principles that have carried me to the very summit of commercial endeavour.

Yet as the minutes tick by and the hand of destiny reaches out, I must bring to a close this verbal banquet that I have laid before you. For time is indeed money. And as stakeholders in this unique venture, you would not thank me for allowing the fleeting indulgences of your chosen leader to stand in the way of the victory that awaits you. I have had the privilege and the honour of leading our company to unprecedented levels of profit. At this auspicious moment in our development we have been given an opportunity for even greater growth and prosperity, an opening so ablaze with the fires of fiscal dominance that even the boldest and most prescient individual among you would never have dared contemplate it in his wildest fantasy.

I would therefore beseech you, fellow voyagers in this epoch-making odyssey, do not become preoccupied with the life-draining minutiae of legal and commercial protocol, but think only of the greater good of your corporation and those, including your good selves, who would look out upon vast new horizons of power and wealth. In commending to you the motion which you have before you, to approve the acquisition of the Comma International Corporation and its subsidiaries, I would reassure those who waver, at the very moment when they should be grasping glorious triumph, that monumental moments such as this are preordained. For there is indeed an order and a meaningfulness to all things. As it is written in the Book of Ecclesiastes, to everything there is a season… a time to be born and a time to die… a time to kill and a time to heal… a time to break down and a time to build up… a time…

The clock in the great hall was poised to chime three o'clock, yet time seemed suddenly to have been suspended as Piers halted dramatically in mid-sentence and stood rooted to the spot, the blood draining from his face, his eyes bulging like a fish stranded on the shore. A frenzied buzz began to ripple across the room as his features froze in a look of pure animal fear. His lips moved but no sound came forth, and as he attempted to swallow the water he had poured into his glass, his hand shook like that of man in the grip of Parkinson's disease.

And what of a time to be kind and long-suffering and loving and generous? The words rang out through the great hall like rifle shots. What of the old-fashioned, decent virtues and motives that in your cold, calculating drive for wealth and power you dismiss as ruthlessly as when you sign the death warrant for a once great and thriving company, tossing aside its employees like last week's garbage? What now my stone-hearted son; what next in your amoral and inhumane drive for profit and self-advancement?

As the audience craned their necks to catch sight of the verbal assailant who had so shockingly appeared at the rear of the hall, the television cameras swooped down on him like giant birds of prey, and the cameras of the paparazzi began to flash and pop as if they were part of some extraordinary light show. The old man himself seemed oblivious to the attention, walking slowly forward along the central gangway towards the podium where Piers stood transfixed, like a rabbit caught in the glare of a car's headlights, still incapable of speech.

As his tormentor shuffled ever closer, Piers could not take in what he was seeing. He tried desperately to convince himself that his mind might in some way have been affected temporarily by the intensity of the occasion and the searing heat of the hall, so packed with people and camera equipment that there was scarcely room to draw breath. Yet he knew that, much as he craved a transitory distortion of his senses to explain away the paralysing presence, which he appeared to be seeing ever more clearly, the figure moving inexorably nearer to him was indeed no apparition.

A few yards from the podium the man came to a halt and gazed full into the face of the one he had come to confront. He was old and stooped like Father Time himself. He leant heavily on his walking stick to support himself, and with his other hand he smoothed back his flowing white hair. The frenzy that had gripped the hall subsided as quickly as it had risen, and in its place came a hush so redolent with highly-charged emotion it was almost tangible. Again Piers tried to speak but no sound came forth. He felt drops of sweat trickling down both temples and moved as if in a dream to wipe his face with the silk monogrammed handkerchief, which had been carefully lodged in the breast pocket of his suit.

What? Is this a mirage I see before me? The old man spoke scornfully in a voice that belied his frail appearance. Can it be that the smooth-tongued – or should that be serpent-tongued – Piers Black is lost for words for the first time in his all-conquering life? Is this not the man who has brought business rivals to their knees, who has single-handedly carried off corporate deals that are the envy of Trump and Murdoch, a man who has world-wide legions of worshippers falling at his feet in admiration?

Oh, great and all-seeing Piers, we are bereft by your sudden loss of voice. We crave so much more of your infinite wisdom. Do not leave us here abandoned like intellectual orphans. Speak to us now of that part of your life of which we, your adoring acolytes, know so little, speak to us now of families.

The old man tossed down his verbal gauntlet with barely concealed disdain. He stood calm and motionless, a faint smile crossing his lips, savouring Piers' complete paralysis. A shaft of sunlight filtering through a window bathed him in a striking translucent glow, and as he finished speaking an eerie silence once again descended over the great hall. The only sound that broke the stillness was the occasional strategic movement of a television camera-man or photographer or a muted cough from an onlooker. The few in the audience who were not transfixed by the surreal but utterly compelling drama being staged in their midst glanced furtively around, monitoring the reaction of their spellbound contemporaries or exchanging looks of stunned disbelief.

What ails you, perfidious Piers? The old man was becoming visibly more self-assured and contemptuous. Could it be that I, who once you acknowledged as your father but who has now become nothing but an irritating blot on your bleak emotional landscape, have found an unsuspected chink in your armour? You stand there resplendent in your fine designer clothes, you drink only the finest champagne and drive the most expensive cars, you own homes in New York, Paris, Monte Carlo and Barbados. Yet there is one thing you lack my erstwhile son, something that flows freely through the veins of men who possess far less material wealth but who know the true value of humanity and humility: the milk of human kindness.

The old man turned to the audience and waved his arm in an expansive gesture towards Piers. Is it any wonder that this crown prince of callous commercial connivance finds no words to say on the subject of families, when he himself has shaken off all ties and concern for his own? He turned back to face Piers again. Your mother and I laboured long and hard to nurture the potential we saw in you, but we sought no thanks for our sacrifice, only the ordinary love and respect of a son for his parents. Yet, venomous Piers, you have spurned us, as a serial philanderer spurns the heartfelt entreaties of his latest conquest. And as for your brothers and sisters, you have betrayed them and disowned them as if they were dross.

And what of those families whose lives will be shattered by the takeover of yet another corporate victim of Piers Black's remorseless drive for world domination? Does he even pause for one split second to give them a thought? Does he see the pain on the faces of those wives whose husbands have been thrust summarily onto the scrapheap or the tears in the eyes of his children when their mother tells them their father has taken his own life because he could not live with the humiliation?

Come now, my fine son, do not be reticent and withholding in this, your finest hour. Reveal to us your thoughts on these seminal matters. We wait in awe and anticipation of your all-knowing response. Speak to us now, we implore you.

As the audience remained mesmerised and Piers still struggled unsuccessfully to find his voice, the television cameras moved in closer, focussing on his tortured features. Then a granite-faced man with the build of a buffalo drew close to Piers and whispered to him: Oh, master of our destiny, shall I rid you of this turbulent pensioner who has disturbed the flow of your genius?

Before Piers could even think of responding, the old man spoke again before turning on his heel and preparing to depart. Fear not, Piers, you have no need of your iron-handed henchmen. I will go now and leave you to your vainglorious posturing, but as you lie between silken sheets in your penthouse tonight think of me and your ailing mother and your siblings, who work like dogs to keep the wolf from the door, and remember the obligations of your birthright. *Noblesse oblige*, my son, but that concept is anathema to your twisted psyche.

As the old man moved towards the door at the rear of the great hall, Piers suddenly found his voice for the first time since the nightmarish figure had appeared before him. Wait! he cried, stepping down from the platform and rushing up behind the retreating figure. He arrived, breathless, at the old man's side just as he was exiting through the oak-beamed portals. I… we… he began in a whisper. We need to… You do not understand… You never understood… You *cannot* understand…

I understand only too well, the old man interjected. In your eyes I see a flicker of something that might once have passed for humanity, yet your soul is as cold as the grave. You hear my words and they have indeed touched that untainted part of you that lingers on deep in your subconscious in spite of yourself. Somewhere inside there is a child who yearns for reconnection and reconciliation with those who nurtured him and valued him before his naked greed and ambition made him into an unfeeling monster, but that child is slowly dying – if he is not already dead. So, my son, though you struggle to find the words, you are incapable of responding to me, because the Piers who came innocently and full of loving promise into this world no longer exists.

I had my reasons, Piers said, reasons you will never comprehend. You are quick to condemn, my sharp-tongued father, but remember the eternal words: Judge not lest ye be judged. The old man looked at him impassively and Piers felt the unfamiliar sensation of tears welling up inside him. He paused momentarily to pull himself together, smoothing his silk tie and methodically brushing tiny pieces of fluff from his suit, fearful that his tangled emotions might show.

Wait. Do not walk away, Piers implored him. It need not end like this. No situation is beyond negotiation. Can we not at least attempt to reach some kind of interim agreement? When this takeover deal has been completed and I stand ready to carry those who sail under my flag to new heights of commercial supremacy, I will arrange for my personal assistant to phone you and fix a meeting.

Negotiation… agreement… pah! the old man snapped. Your mind is fatally flawed. Even now, when your inner man that has lain dormant for so long is screaming at you to do the decent thing, your lust for power and profit brushes everything aside like a sandstorm in the desert. Finance before family; it was ever thus, and it will be that way until you die. Whoever said blood is thicker than water did not have Piers Black in mind. In your case blood means nothing, unless it is the blood of corporate opponents spilled in futile attempts to fend off the inevitable.

Go back to your world, Piers, the old man continued. You do not belong in ours. I came to bring the mighty Piers down to earth, to see if that flickering flame of decency might yet be rekindled, but I was hopelessly misguided. I can see it in your eyes, as cold and soulless as the surface of the moon. You are what you are, nothing more, nothing less. I do not even despise you. I pity you. When you are old and wizened like me, will your millions warm your calloused heart as you contemplate senility and death? Will the women you have conquered and cast aside, like so many playthings, rush to comfort you as you struggle for breath? Will all your companies and your fine penthouses and your cars be able to save your blackened soul?

The old man raised his hand in a mock salute. Adieu, oh great and all-powerful Piers. You are indeed as rich as Croesus, but your spirit is as impoverished as the lowliest pauper. To paraphrase your own twisted logic, you know the price of everything but the value of nothing. And that in the end, my avaricious son, will be your downfall.

Piers tried to speak as the stooped figure turned and shuffled through the door, but again the words would not come. As the old man disappeared from view, he thought he heard a cackle like that of the old harridan who had harangued him before the meeting began, but when he turned to look there was no one in sight. As he did so, the clock in the great hall chimed three times and he felt a chill run down the entire length of his spine.

His mind was on overload, his heart pounding like a piledriver. Cold fear seemed to be draining the life-force from his body as he contemplated a nightmare vision of the future. Had the old witch been right? Had his father succeeded where countless commercial adversaries had failed? Would he, *could* he ever be the same again? He was brought suddenly to his senses by a phalanx of television and radio interviewers homing in on him like wasps round a sugar bowl. Mr Black! Mr Black! they implored. Who *was* that man? Was he really your father? How long is it since you last saw him? What about the rest of your family?

Piers glanced uncertainly around and, for a moment, he wanted to run from the room like a small child in a school assembly singled out by the headmaster. He felt like an impostor, a monstrous fraud whose cover has been blown. How could he explain away the poison darts from his father that had cut so deep and left him so exposed and, above all, revealed the tainted legacy of his birth? Yet as he stood there, hesitantly, tasting the unfamiliar pangs of indecision and doubt, he perceived the awe and the adulation that still burned in the eyes of those who surrounded him, craving one word from his lips as a junkie craves the needle, and he knew he still held the ultimate source of power in his manicured hands.

Slowly he felt the glow of confidence beginning to wash over him again. The dense cloud of confusion that had paralysed his normally unshakeable capacity for logical thought was lifting like a young bride's veil as she kneels before the altar. As a young female reporter thrust her microphone in front of his face and began to mouth a question, he smiled at her, then waved her and the pursuing pack of eager hacks away.

Ladies and gentlemen of the media, I thank you for your concern, but I have nothing to say to you at this time. I have a meeting to conduct and a deal of global significance to push through. So, if you will excuse me…

Like a lion rousing itself from its post-prandial slumber, Piers strode purposefully back to the platform. He looked slowly and imperiously around the room, banged several times on the lectern with the gavel to bring the meeting to order and began to speak.

Ladies and gentlemen, fellow shareholders, the sideshow is at an end. The poor misguided individual you saw disappearing in the same shoddy manner as he arrived is as deluded as he is pathetic and, in my magnanimity, I will not seek retribution for his unseemly disruption. Indeed, though time presses even more strongly than before, I will honour his request and speak to you of families.

Like a great actor playing to his public, he paused for dramatic effect to survey the audience hanging once again on every syllable coming from his lips. And though inside he was still feeling the lingering turmoil from the ferocity of his father's attack, he knew he would overcome the transitory crisis as surely as the sun would rise over the Square Mile the next morning.

For in retrospect, he told himself, is it not good that I have confronted and overcome the ultimate demon that has stalked my subconscious like an avenging angel for so long? As Kipling has written, if you can meet with Triumph and Disaster and treat those two impostors just the same, you will indeed be a man, my son. And as my opponents know only too well, I am no ordinary man. My greatness is written in the annals of time and it cannot be unhinged by the fickle hand of fate that determined my base and incongruous origins.

And he spoke to them with an assurance that grew with each and every carefully chosen word he uttered: Families are the great lie, the great delusion, the great impostor who comes with honeyed words and drains the very fountain of life. They are the glue that bonds and sticks as a limpet clings fast to the bottom of a ship; they are the silken thread that binds by cruel accident of birth and suffocates as surely and irresistibly as the boa constrictor crushes his prey. They are the universal hope of man and the despair of all mankind; they hold the eternal promise of deliverance and deliver nothing but the bitter sting of empty longing.

For what is a family but a hapless body of diverse individuals thrown together by a quirk of fate that is as unpredictable and capricious as the wind? And why is it that people possessed of personalities, characteristics and ambitions that are as different and unique as fingerprints must go through the great sham of masquerading as one? And whilst the love a mother feels for her child is as real and unchanging as the orbit of the planets around the sun, yet is the expectancy of love and esteem between family members who revile and abuse one another as false and valueless as a forger's copy of an old master.

And though the experts would perpetuate the myth that families are pivotal in the nurture of the individual and their growth towards wholeness and emotional maturity, is it not true that Freud and his successors have shown that they are also the foundation stone of all neuroses and psychological ills? And is it not also true that human dross as malevolent and divisive as the Mafia call themselves family? And do not even reptiles and vermin and all the most unsavoury creatures that crawl on this earth have families, too?

And as Piers glanced at his diamond-encrusted Rolex, he flashed a smile of self-satisfaction, before continuing: And now, as time presses heavily, it is with ultimate regard for our corporate clan, the only type of family that offers true riches and enlightenment, that I exhort you to follow me along the path that eternity has set before us. Fellow profit-seekers, we are at the epicentre of the commerce-time continuum. At this seminal moment in business history we hold the key to greatness in the palm of our hands. And in the final accounting, when all the eloquent words and utterances have been spoken, it comes down to this: you know me, you know my track record writ large in figures of unparalleled profitability. And therefore, ladies and gentlemen, there is only one conclusion: you are either with me or against me.

And he knew in his heart which way they would go, and his spirit was once again filled with a singular kind of joy. And as he prepared to sign and seal the most audacious and far-reaching deal of his extraordinary young life, he knew in that moment that destiny had claimed him for its own.

ALSO AVAILABLE IN THE GREAT LITTLE READS SERIES

THE CLOVERLEAF DEVELOPMENT
KEITH SCALES

SELLING LIGHT
EFFIE GRAY

LIZARD
L. SCHICK

CHURCHTOWN
ANTHONY CALESHU

LITTLE ROASTS
COLLECTION OF STORIES